TEN MILE VALLEY

TEN MILE VALLEY

A Western Story

WAYNE D. OVERHOLSER

Skyhorse Publishing

Skyhorse Publishing books may be purchased in bulk at special discounts for sales promotion, corporate gifts, fund-raising, or educational purposes. Special editions can also be created to specifications. For details, contact the Special Sales Department, Skyhorse Publishing, 307 West 36th Street, 11th Floor, New York, NY 10018 or info@skyhorsepublishing.com.

Skyhorse® and Skyhorse Publishing® are registered trademarks of Skyhorse Publishing, Inc.®, a Delaware corporation.

Visit our website at www.skyhorsepublishing.com.

10 9 8 7 6 5 4 3 2 1

Library of Congress Cataloging-in-Publication Data is available on file.

Cover design by Brian Peterson

Print ISBN: 978-1-63450-747-9
Ebook ISBN: 978-1-63450-748-6

Printed in the United States of America

Chapter One

Tomorrow was the day, the day Mark Kelton had dreamed about for weeks. Now he couldn't sleep. He lay on his back, staring at the dark sky and listening to the Deschutes whisper to him as it ran north to the Columbia: *Tomorrow you'll be in Prineville and you'll see the ranch your father is going to buy on Ochoco Creek.*

At eighteen Mark was part boy, part man—boy enough to live in his dreams, man enough to do a day's work. It was his dreams that kept him awake. He'd be a cowboy. He'd have his own horse and saddle. He'd wear a gun. There were rattlesnakes in central Oregon. Indians maybe. Even outlaws. These were the things of which dreams were made, and they rolled through his head, each a little more exciting than the one before.

He could hear his father's snores from the wagon where he slept with Mark's mother. Beside him was a box with $8,000 in it, the results of the sale of their Willamette Valley farm, enough to buy the ranch on the Ochoco and pay expenses until the ranch gave them a living.

"It ain't going to be like farming in the Willamette Valley," Mark's father had told his wife. "We'll have to learn ranching just like you learn anything new."

"I don't see why you're bound to go," she'd said. "We're getting along all right."

"Growing webs between our toes," his father'd snorted. "Rain and mud. I tell you, Martha, I'm getting tired of it. It's different once you get across the mountains. A mite cold maybe, but 'most every day you see the sun. Makes you feel like tearing the bone out."

"There's Indians," she'd said. "Look at what happened to Custer."

"Oh, Martha, be sensible. That was a thousand miles from here." He'd caught her hands and brought her to him, not knowing Mark was watching. "The Willamette Valley's old country. Settled twenty, thirty years ago. A lot of it's worn out, but it's different on the other side of the mountains. If you don't like the ranch I looked at, we'll buy another one. Or go up the creek and homestead. It's a big country. If we go now, we can take our pick of the land."

"I hate to have Mark . . ."

"Mark's the reason we've got to go. Here a man's smothered. Crowded in with farms all around him, but over there we'll grow with the country."

She hadn't argued any more. They had sold the farm and loaded a covered wagon and started out. Up the Santiam. The long climb to the top of Seven Mile Hill. Clear Lake, where they stayed two days and fished, the water so clear that snags of trees hundreds of feet below in the bottom of the lake looked as if their tops were just under the surface.

Every day had been an adventure for Mark. He had never seen timber like this, giant firs crowding the road. Sometimes from a high point he had seen one tree-covered ridge after another, running on and on into infinity until the very beauty of it became monotonous.

He shivered and pulled his blankets up under his chin. It was chilly, even in July. He wished he could go to sleep. They'd be up before dawn, for it was still most of a day's journey to Prineville. Maybe they wouldn't see the ranch tomorrow. They might stay in town overnight and rent a buggy and drive up the creek the next morning.

Camping out had pleasured Mark and his father, but not his mother. She was anxious to get settled again, and, if the ranch house was well built, with the windows and doors tight against the weather, Mark knew she wouldn't object to buying the place. He thought he heard something in the brush downriver and sat up, trembling. He listened, but he heard nothing more. Some animal prowling for food. Maybe a bear. Well, there was nothing to worry about.

An Indian? The thought sent a little prickle down his spine. The Malheur reservation wasn't far to the east, and Mark had heard about the Snake renegade, Pablito, who had cut a bloody path through this country not long ago. He considered waking his father, but he'd just be laughed at and told to go back to sleep. The fire was only a dull eye in the darkness. He should build it up again, but he didn't want to leave his warm bed. A moment later he dropped off to sleep.

He didn't know what woke him. Some sound. He had the feeling he'd heard a scream, but now there was only silence. It must have been a nightmare. Still, he could not rid himself of the terrifying feeling that something was wrong. The fire was completely out. There was a faint glow of star shine on the water, like the thin glint of lamplight caught on the surface of obsidian. Suddenly the night came alive with noise. A groan from inside the wagon. The slithering sound of someone slipping out of the wagon. A man's heavy voice: "I found it."

Mark caught the faint blur of movement. He threw off the blankets in a wild sweep and charged at the intruder, wanting to yell a warning to his parents, but his throat was so tight he couldn't make a sound. He smashed into the man, a fist striking out wildly. It grazed the fellow's chin, the back of his hand scraping across a tough, wiry beard. He lost his balance and fell forward. The man grunted an oath. Mark felt a sharp corner jab him in the ribs. Stars exploded in front of him as someone smashed him across the head with a gun barrel. Then he fell down in the grass.

* * * * *

When Mark came to, the sun was fully up above the eastern rim. He raised himself by his arms, his head aching with great, pulsating throbs. He dropped back into the grass, sick at the stomach. He called: "Ma!" No answer. He shouted: "Pa!" Still no answer. He gripped the spokes of a front wheel and pulled himself upright, holding to the wheel until the worst of the dizziness passed.

He looked into the wagon. A sound was choked out of him, a strangled, incoherent sound. He shut his eyes tight, thinking he was still having the nightmare he'd thought he was having when he woke during the night. But when he opened his eyes, he saw the same thing.

His parents were dead. Stabbed! Blood was all over the inside of the wagon, on the blankets half covering his father and mother. Their eyes were open; blood had dried and turned brown on their skin. He made himself crawl inside and touch their faces. He recoiled in horror, a clammy feeling knotting his insides and momentarily stopping his breathing.

He clambered out of the wagon and started to run. He fell and for a time lay there, breathing hard, then he got up and ran again. There was no purpose in him, no direction. He just ran. Afterward he could not remember anything about the next hour. He followed the road to where it started to climb to the rim, then he couldn't run any more. He lay in the dust, sobbing for breath.

He was still there when someone asked: "What's the matter, son?"

He turned his head. A man on a roan horse, a tall man with a heavy black mustache, the skin of his long face turned leather-brown by wind and sun. He sat his saddle easily in the manner of a man who spends more time on a horse than on the ground.

Mark sat up and tried to say something, but the words stuck in his throat. The man swung out of the saddle and, letting his reins drag, squatted in the dust beside Mark. He said, his voice gentle: "You look like the last day in hell, boy. What happened?"

"Ma. Pa." Mark wet his cracked lips. "They've been murdered."

"Murdered?" The man grinned. "Somebody gave you the wrong brand of whiskey, son. Nobody gets murdered in this country. Nothing worth murdering for except horses, and a horse thief gets strung up so fast that the bad ones figger it ain't worth it."

"They're dead." Mark wet his lips again. "Stabbed."

The man's grin died. "Horses gone?"

"I didn't look. There was a box inside the wagon. Had $8,000 in it."

"Eight thousand dollars." The man whistled. "There ain't that much money in central Oregon. Where'd your pa get it?"

"Sold his farm. He was going to buy a ranch near Prineville."

The man rolled a cigarette, watching Mark closely. "I'll go take a look," he said finally. "You stay here. Your pa have a saddle horse?"

Mark nodded. "A sorrel."

"I'll saddle him and fetch him back with me. There's a ranch yonder." He motioned toward the rim. "I'd best take you there." He mounted and looked down at Mark. "Get into the shade and stay here. Savvy? This is a big country and damned few people."

Mark nodded and watched the man turn his horse and ride away. He dragged himself to a pine and sat with his back to the trunk. His head still ached, and he was so tired he wasn't sure he could ever move again, but he was over the worst of the shock, enough to know this was no nightmare. It had happened. His folks were dead. He had no one to turn to, no place to go.

Chapter Two

Half an hour later the man returned, leading the sorrel. His face was grave. "I thought you had a touch of sun, but it's just like you said. Mount up, boy. I'll take you to the Baxes' place, then I'll go back and fetch the wagon."

Mark obeyed mechanically. They started up the narrow road to the rim, Mark riding with his head down, one hand clutching the horn. Presently the man said: "I'm Bronco Curtis. What's your name, son?"

"Mark Kelton."

"Where were you from?"

"We had a farm near Albany."

Curtis glanced at Mark and was silent. They crossed a sage-covered ridge and dropped down into a small valley. Curtis motioned to the buildings ahead of them. "This is the Baxes' place. They're good people. They'll look after you."

Judged by the buildings, it wasn't much of a ranch: a log cabin, a shed, and a pole corral. Mark wondered if the place on the Ochoco his father had planned to buy was like this one. There wasn't even a woodshed. A pile of pine limbs and small stuff, more like brush than anything else, lay back of the cabin, a chopping block and an axe beside it.

A woman was hanging up clothes on a line between two juniper trees. Curtis said—"Good morning, Missus Baxes"—and, stepping down, walked toward her, skirting the white-crusted spot in front of the door where she threw her wash water.

Mrs. Baxes was a big woman, heavy of breast and wide of hips. She wiped her hands on a dirty apron and shook hands with Curtis. "Ain't seen you for a 'coon's age, Bronco," she said. "Where you been?"

"Around," he said, and lowering his voice went on talking.

Mrs. Baxes listened, shocked by what he told her. Then she said: "Fred's out in the shed. Tell him about it. Sure, we'll look out for the boy."

She walked to Mark and, reaching up, patted him on the arm. "Bronco told me about your folks. I'm sure sorry. Don't seem like anything that bad could really happen. Now you go unsaddle and put your horse in the corral, then come in and I'll fix you some breakfast."

"I'm not hungry," Mark said.

"You'd best eat something," she said. "Go take care of your horse."

He obeyed, and, when he went into the cabin, Mrs. Baxes was standing at the stove, frying several pieces of fatty salt side. She said: "Sit down, I'm heating up the coffee. It'll be ready in a minute."

Mark sat down on a bench at a rough pine table. The cabin had a dirt floor. There were several benches, a bed opposite the stove, a crate that served as a dressing table, and a few shelves beside the stove, which were filled with cans and sacks of food.

An offensive stench permeated the room, a combination of sweat and filth and grease that must have accumulated for years. He knew what his mother would have said if she were here. *No use to try cleaning up a place like this. You've just got to burn it down.*

He wondered if the ranch house on the Ochoco was like this. His mother would have sat down and cried if it had been. She'd fought dirt as long as Mark could remember. Most of the spankings she'd given him had been for forgetting to clean his shoes before he went into the house. He remembered how she'd looked, lying in the wagon, blood all over her and her mouth sagging open and the glassy expression of her eyes. Then he couldn't stand it any longer, and he put his head down on his arms and began to cry.

Mrs. Baxes brought him a plate with the salt side and three soggy biscuits. She put an arm around him and hugged him. "Now, now, don't do no good to cry. Nothing will bring 'em back, but maybe we'll find the varmint that done it."

He sat up, and wiped a sleeve across his eyes. He hadn't meant to cry. He stared at his plate while Mrs. Baxes poured a cup of black coffee for him.

"Bronco went after the wagon," she said. "Fred, that's my husband, is digging the graves on the ridge yonder. We got a baby buried up there. Only baby we ever had and there won't be no more." She put an arm around him again. "You see, you ain't the only one who's got trouble."

"I can't eat anything," he said. "I'm sorry I put you to so much bother for nothing."

"Pshaw, now, it wasn't no bother," she said. "You got any other folks? A brother or sister or just anybody?"

"Nobody."

"You don't mind burying your folks here, do you, son? It's too long a trip back to the Willamette Valley, and Prineville wouldn't be no better than here."

"No, its all right." He got up. "I'll go help dig the graves."

He found Fred Baxes working inside a small fenced enclosure. Baxes straightened up and wiped his forehead on his sleeve when he saw Mark. He was a scrawny, long-necked man with dribbles of tobacco juice running down both sides of his chin. He held out a hand, and Mark took it.

"I'm Fred Baxes. Bronco, he told me what happened. I'm sure sorry. Hard to believe such a thing could happen right next door, you might say."

"My name's Mark Kelton." He motioned toward the grave Baxes had started. "I'd like to help."

"There's another shovel in the shed. Be glad to have your help."

Mark fetched the shovel from the shed, and, when he returned, he saw the little grave with a board marked:

BABY BAXES

1 DAY OLD

No, he wasn't the only one with trouble, but their trouble didn't make his any easier.

The soil was sandy and inclined to run back into the graves. There were rocks, too, and some of them so big that it took both Baxes and Mark to lift them to the top. Neither of them talked. Then, after they were done, Baxes said: "I'll fix up a couple of boards. Maybe someday you'll come back and put up some stone markers." Mark nodded, and Baxes asked: "What was your folks' names?"

"Leonard Kelton." Mark had to fight back the tears before he could add: "Martha Kelton."

He followed Baxes to the shed, where the rancher found a board that he sawed in two. Taking out his pocket knife, he carved a name upon each half. Bronco Curtis came with the wagon, and Mark took care of the horses. Curtis found some canvas in the wagon, and he and Baxes wrapped the bodies in it and carried them to the graves. Mark stayed at the corral. Presently Curtis and Baxes returned.

"Want to look at your folks before the burying?" Curtis asked.

Mark shook his head.

"All right, we'd better get at it."

"I'll get Amy," Baxes said, and went on to the cabin.

Mark walked up the ridge with Curtis. Baxes and his wife came a moment later, Mrs. Baxes carrying a Bible. The men took off their hats, then Mrs. Baxes read the Twenty-Third Psalm and said the Lord's Prayer.

Mark looked up at the sky. The days were never as clear as this in the Willamette Valley, where there were always clouds, or at least a haze in the air. Here the sky held a strange, depthless blue. Mark wondered if God was up there, and would He let Mark's parents into heaven without a preacher to pray for them?

He watched while Curtis and Baxes filled the graves. He helped lift the rocks onto the sandy dirt to keep it from blowing, then Baxes slipped the markers into place at the heads of the graves. They walked back down the slope, and, when they reached the cabin, Mark said: "There should have been a preacher."

"There ain't none hereabouts," Mrs. Baxes said. "We didn't have one when Baby died."

"It isn't like it was where you lived," Curtis said. "Over here folks make out by themselves."

"I reckon God don't mind," Mrs. Baxes said. "He's with us all the time. I guess we live closer to Him than folks do on the other side of the mountains." She looked at Mark. "Know what you're going to do, son?"

"I can't go back," Mark said. "Nothing to go back to." He tried to swallow the lump in his throat, but it wouldn't go down. "I'll saddle up and go to Prineville. Maybe I can find a job."

"We'd like to have you stay here," Mrs. Baxes said. "Like I told you, we won't never have no children. Stay with us and help Fred with the work and . . . and be our son."

Mark dug his toe through the dirt, staring at it. His chest hurt. They were good, Amy and Fred Baxes and Bronco Curtis. He didn't know what he would have done without them, but he couldn't stay. He couldn't tell Mrs. Baxes the truth, though, about the dirty house and the smell and everything.

"He don't have to decide right now," Bronco Curtis said.

"No, of course he don't," Mrs. Baxes said. "I'll go fix dinner."

"Thank you kindly," Mark said, "but I can't stay here. I guess it's too close to where they're buried. I just can't."

Mrs. Baxes nodded. "I reckon I understand. I just wanted you to know you're welcome."

She went into the house.

Curtis said: "You've got the wagon and the team besides the sorrel. You've got some real good furniture in the wagon. Now, it don't look to me like you can live in it. Maybe you could sell the outfit in Prineville. Might be you could get a job on a ranch. During haying, anyhow. After that, you'd know better about what you want to do."

Mark looked at Baxes, thinking about the crude, home-made furniture in the cabin. He said impulsively: "You take it. I can't go driving the wagon all over the country."

"Hold on," Curtis said. "You can't give your whole outfit away. You need a little money and . . ."

"He can have it," Mark said, thinking of the skinny team he had seen in the corral.

Curtis threw up his hands. "It's your rig, but . . ."

"I'll give you all the money I've got," Baxes said eagerly. "I don't need the wagon, and we can get along with the furniture we've got, but I sure could use a good team. You get anything you need out of the wagon, and I'll fetch your money."

Curtis walked beside Mark to the wagon. He said: "You're a fool, kid. You could get three, four hundred dollars out of this outfit in Prineville."

Mark didn't say anything. He crawled into the wagon. Dark splotches of blood stained the bed. He tried not to look at it. He got his father's rifle, a box of shells, the cartridge belt and holster, and the bone-handled .44 Colt. He found a clean shirt, a pair of pants, and some socks, and stuffed them into a sack, then took a side of bacon and some biscuits from the grub box and put them into the sack too.

Curtis was still scowling when Mark stepped down beside him. As Mark started to buckle the gun belt around him, Curtis said: "You ever shoot that revolver?"

Mark nodded. "Once."

"That's what I thought," Curtis said. "This ain't your kind of country, kid. You'd better understand that now. You wear that iron into Prineville and some other kid will decide to find out if you can use it and you'll be dead."

Mark rubbed his forehead. His head was throbbing so bad he couldn't think. "What'll I do with it?"

"Wrap it in your slicker and carry it behind the saddle. You'll have the rifle in the boot. Use it to shoot any game you need."

Baxes came out of the cabin, a small sack in his hand. "This is all I've got, $32.47." He wiped the back of a hand across his mouth. "Amy says for you to come and eat."

Mark took the money and shoved it into his pocket. Curtis wheeled away, disgusted. They went into the cabin and sat down at the table, Mrs. Baxes pouring the coffee. She'd warmed up the biscuits and had fried antelope steak. Mark couldn't eat, but he drank his coffee.

When the rest finished, Mark rose. "I'll saddle my horse." He fought the lump in his throat, and finally managed: "Thank you."

"God bless you, Mark," Mrs. Baxes said, and kissed him. "Don't forget now. If you change your mind, you come on back."

Mark stumbled out of the cabin, not wanting them to see he had started to cry again. He saddled the sorrel and rolled the gun belt and revolver into the slicker, then tied it and the sack behind the saddle. He didn't know Curtis was there until the man's big hands appeared beside his.

"Let me do that," he said. "Hell, kid, you'd lose the whole works before you'd gone half a mile."

Mark stepped back and watched while Curtis pulled the leather thongs tight. He said—"Thanks."—and climbed awkwardly into the saddle.

"I'll ride along with you," Curtis said. "You might get lost between here and Prineville. I reckon we'd better tell the deputy over there what happened."

Mark waited while Curtis saddled and mounted. They rode away, Mark waving at Fred Baxes and his wife, who was dabbing at her eyes with a handkerchief.

Curtis was silent until they dropped over the ridge and the Baxes place was out of sight, then he turned to Mark, his face dark with suppressed anger. "Just thirty-two bucks! They're trash, kid, just trash. They'll never get ahead. They'll live on that rock pile and starve to death the rest of their lives. Why in hell did you do it?"

Mark rubbed his forehead again. It was still aching. He looked down at the sagebrush through which his horse was traveling. He shivered, even with the hot afternoon sun pressing down upon his back. Finally he said: "I guess it was because they were good to me."

He was afraid Curtis was going to say more, but the man let it drop. He glanced up at the sun that was low in the west, and said: "We won't get to Prineville before dark. Reckon we better swing back to the river and camp."

Mark took a long breath that was almost a sob. At least he wouldn't be alone tonight.

Chapter Three

They reached Prineville shortly after noon, tied their horses in front of a restaurant, and went in and ordered dinner. Mark had ridden a good deal, but never for more than an hour or two at a time, and now he discovered he was so sore he could hardly stand the hard seat of the bench at the table.

Curtis noticed, and grinned. "You'll get over it. After a while you'll be able to sit a saddle from sunup to sundown and do it day after day."

"Maybe I'd make out better if I walked."

"Not if you're going to stay in this country," Curtis said. "Ain't like the Willamette Valley. People ride, either on a horse or behind one. That's why a horse thief gets sentenced soon as he's caught."

Their dinners came and Curtis ate with noisy gusto. Mark still found it hard to eat. Everything seemed tasteless. He tried not to think about his parents, tried to keep from seeing them in his mind as he had seen them yesterday morning, but the ghastly scene kept slipping back. More than once during the ride from the Deschutes tears had suddenly filled his eyes and run down his cheeks.

He always turned his head quickly so Curtis wouldn't see the tears. He couldn't help it, he told himself defiantly. He didn't care. Bronco Curtis could think anything he wanted to.

But he did care. Right now he wanted Curtis's respect more than anything in the world, and he knew he didn't have it. Selling his team and wagon to Fred Baxes for $32.47 had made him look like a fool in Curtis's eyes. But it was his business, Mark told himself. He still wasn't sorry about it.

His prospects worried him more than anything else. He couldn't live very long on $32.47. He could sell his father's rifle and the Colt, then the saddle and the sorrel, but what would he do then?

He could do a man's work in the field. He was five feet, ten inches tall; he weighed one hundred and fifty-two pounds, and judged by what was considered a day's work in the Willamette Valley, he could hold his own with any man. But it was a tougher country on this side of the mountains. Even if he was lucky and got a job, haying wouldn't last long. What would he do then?

He pushed his plate back and watched Curtis pour coffee into his saucer and drink it. Mark had never met a man like him. He was twenty-three, or so he said last night when they were eating supper, but he looked older. Maybe it was because he had been making his living since he was ten. He had made a point of that to Mark.

There was little sympathy from him, now that Mark's parents had been buried and the amenities that the tragedy demanded had been met. There was no softness in him. More than once Mark had glanced at him during the ride to Prineville and found his dark face strangely bitter and forbidding, as if he harbored thoughts that he found profoundly disturbing.

Mark sensed a great strength about Curtis, a strength Mark's father had never possessed. Perhaps it was a quality this country demanded of its people. If a man didn't have it, he didn't survive. He must be like the junipers, and the sage and rabbitbrush, and the bare rimrock that frightened Mark because there was nothing like it in the Willamette Valley with its round buttes and lush grass and timbered hills.

Mark could be sure of only one thing. Bronco Curtis would meet any emergency that came up. If Mark could be with him for a while, he would learn the things he had to know to live in eastern Oregon and this was where he wanted to live. But Curtis hadn't indicated what he was going to do or where he was going. He hadn't hinted that he'd put up with Mark after today, either.

Mark had too much pride to force himself upon Curtis. That was one of the things his father had taught him. *If a man doesn't meet you at least a quarter of the way, he doesn't want you around. If you push it, he'll give you nothing but trouble.*

Curtis finished eating and, leaning back in his chair, belched with satisfaction. "This is on me," he said. He walked to the counter and paid for both meals. When they were outside, he nodded at the Red Front Livery Stable. "The deputy is Bud Ackerman. He runs the stable yonder. He ain't much of a lawman, but he's all there is in this end of the county."

Mark crossed the street, thinking it was queer that Curtis hadn't said he was going to be around. But he hadn't said he was leaving right now, either. When Mark reached the archway of the stable, he glanced back. Curtis was leaning against the hitch pole, rolling a cigarette, his gaze on a saloon on the other side of the street.

Mark found Ackerman in his office. He looked up when Mark stopped in the doorway. He asked: "What can I do for you, bub?"

"You're the deputy?"

"Yes, sir, I'm the deputy." Ackerman glanced at the star pinned to his vest and polished it with his sleeve. "I'm all the law there is hereabouts. Got a complaint?"

"My parents were murdered night before last."

Ackerman's arm dropped away from his vest, his eyes skeptical. "Where's the bodies?"

"Buried at the Baxes' place."

"What's your name?"

"Mark Kelton."

"What was your pa's name?"

"Leonard Kelton. He had $8,000 in a metal box in the wagon. He was coming here to buy the Barnes Ranch up Ochoco Creek."

"I remember him," Ackerman said. "He was here last fall looking around, wasn't he?" Mark nodded, and Ackerman added: "It's a pity. He was the kind of man we need in this country." He reached for his pipe and filled it. "How'd it happen?"

Mark told him everything he could remember, then Ackerman said: "This fellow had a beard, and, when you fell against him, you felt something sharp. Must have been the box with the money."

"I guess so."

"But you didn't get a look at him? You couldn't identify him if you seen him?"

"No, sir, I couldn't."

Ackerman snapped his pipe stem against his teeth, his eyes on the ceiling. "Well, bub, I'll go over and take a look, but it ain't likely I'll pick up any tracks after all this time and Curtis sashaying around there like he done. Chances are the killer's two hundred miles from here by now, and there ain't no way on God's green earth of telling which way he went." He looked at Mark as he said reprovingly: "You should o' come here and told me right off."

"Yes, sir," Mark said, and thought that was a fool thing for Ackerman to say, knowing Mark was new to the country.

"I'll ride over there first thing in the morning," Ackerman said. "Meanwhile I'll be thinking on it." He cuddled the bowl of his pipe in his hand and stared at it. "The killer must have followed your wagon all the way from Albany. Nobody would figger there was that kind of money in a wagon. It was foolishment for your pa to be packing so much."

"Barnes told him to fetch cash."

"That'd be like Lafe Barnes," Ackerman said. "But Lafe didn't know he was coming, did he?"

"Pa wrote a letter to him, but he didn't say when he'd get here."

"Wasn't Lafe, even if he did know. He was right here in town playing poker till three o'clock in the morning." Ackerman scratched his cheek. "I can't figger why the killer waited till your folks was clean over here on the Deschutes, unless he didn't want to do it in Linn County, with a regular sheriff there in Albany. Or maybe he knew he could make a getaway faster over here where there ain't many people and nobody likely to see him. I'll talk to Fred Baxes, but he won't know nothing."

Ackerman laid his pipe on the desk. "This here Bronco Curtis now. Kind o' funny, him showing up like he done, so quick an' all."

"He was camped three miles down the river. He wouldn't have come the way he did if he'd been the one."

"No, reckon he wouldn't," Ackerman conceded. "Well, you run along, son. Like I said, I'll ride out there in the morning."

Mark left the stable, convinced that Ackerman would never find the killer. The only other lawman Mark had ever seen was old Baldy Bridges, an Albany policeman who stood on the street every Saturday afternoon and visited with the farmers when they came to town. Mark had often heard his father say that Baldy couldn't have caught a fly that settled on his nose on a fall afternoon if its feet had been dipped in molasses.

Bud Ackerman was no better, Mark thought, and that bothered him because he expected something better in this country. The hard truth was the killer would never be caught, not unless Mark did it himself, and there was no use fooling himself about what he could do. Two years from now, or even one . . .

He was halfway across the street when he realized that Curtis was arguing with a man in front of the restaurant. Curtis was angry, so angry his lips were white, and he raised his voice to a shout: "By God, Red, can't you get it through your thick skull that I ain't going with you? We're done. Finished. Haven't you got sense enough to savvy that?"

The other man was big, so big he seemed to dwarf Curtis, who stood not more than two paces in front of him. He laughed, a great belly laugh that shook his huge body. His hat was pushed back, a lock of red hair showing against his forehead. Mark stopped, flat-footed, his heart pounding so hard it seemed to be coming out of his chest. The redhead had a beard, a short, wiry beard.

"You got yourself worked up into quite a lather, now ain't you, Bronco?" the redhead said. "You best cool off before I soak your head in the horse trough yonder." It was a deep voice, the same voice Mark had heard yesterday morning when it had said: *I found it.* A strangled cry came out of Mark's throat. He ran toward his sorrel and tried to jerk the rifle out of the boot, but he was all thumbs. Somehow he got it into a bind and it stuck.

"Ackerman!" Mark yelled. "Ackerman! He's out here! Come and get him!"

He had the rifle out then, and whirled toward the redhead. He stopped and stood dead still, the rifle pointed at the ground. The redhead had wheeled to face him, his fingers wrapped around the butt of his gun. In that instant Mark knew he had been very close to death. Bronco Curtis had rammed the muzzle of his revolver into the small of the redhead's back. That, and that alone, had kept the redhead from blasting life out of Mark while he was yelling for Ackerman and tugging at his rifle.

"Damn it, put that rifle back!" Curtis ordered. He said something in a low voice to the redhead who started across the street on a run to a big black gelding that had been tied in front of a saloon. "That ain't your man, Mark," Curtis said. "We were camped together that night."

Mark remained motionless, the rifle in his hands. Curtis's revolver was on Mark. Then he saw the hesitation that held Mark motionless, and he whirled to cover the redhead, who was in the saddle. Again he saved Mark's life, for the redhead had his gun high in the air and was chopping down for a shot at Mark.

Curtis threw a shot that must have come within inches of the big man's face. "Get out of town, you fool!" Curtis yelled. "Get out before I kill you!"

The redhead needed no more urging. He left on a dead run. Ackerman, in the street in front of the stable, jumped back and sprawled in the dust. If he hadn't moved fast, he would have been run down by the black horse. He scrambled up, cursing as other men ran into the street.

Curtis walked toward Ackerman. "Sorry about the excitement. The kid just went off half-cocked. That's all."

Ackerman wiped his face with his hands, fingers leaving long streaks of dirt. The others gathered around him—a bartender, a barber, a storekeeper, a couple of cowboys, all of them puzzled by what had happened.

"I heard what the kid said." Ackerman glared at Curtis. "What'd you let that *hombre* go for?"

"I said he wasn't the one." Curtis held his gun at his side now, but there was no doubt from the expression on his face that he'd use it if Ackerman pushed. Ackerman did not push.

The bartender asked: "What was the shooting about?"

"I was hurrying Malone out of town," Curtis said.

"What was you in such a damned big hurry for?" Ackerman asked. "If he was the wrong man."

"I've seen what happens to men when wild talk gets started," Curtis said. "I didn't aim to see Malone hang. That's all. I told you, and I won't tell you again. The kid was mistaken. Malone wasn't the man. We were camped together, and I was up a couple of times during the night. Malone never left his blankets."

"Why would the kid be wrong?" Ackerman asked. "If he recognized Malone's voice . . . ?"

"Oh, hell," Curtis said. "He didn't. You can't remember exactly what a voice sounds like. Anyhow, the kid had been asleep, and he naturally got excited when he jumped the killer. The only thing he's sure about is that the fellow had a beard. When he left the stable, he saw Malone's beard. Well, there's a lot of beards in the country, Ackerman. The kid just made a wrong guess."

Curtis wheeled and strode across the street to his horse. "Let's get moving, Mark,"—he said loudly, and added in a low voice— "before they think you done it."

Mark jammed the rifle into the boot, completely confused, and untied the sorrel. As he stepped into the saddle, Ackerman called: "How about it, bub? Was it like the gent says?"

"I guess it was," Mark answered. "I saw his beard and started hollering."

Mark swung the sorrel and put him into a gallop. He caught up with Curtis, dust rolling up behind them, but even then he wasn't sure. The redhead's voice sounded exactly like the voice that had said: *I found it.*

Chapter Four

They camped on the Crooked River that night. Prineville was ten miles downstream from them. Mark kept his worry and fear bottled up until they staked out the horses and built a fire. Then he burst out: "You don't think anybody would believe I killed my own parents?"

"Why not?" Curtis was slicing bacon into a frying pan. "I reckon any of us would do 'most anything for $8,000."

"I wouldn't!" Mark cried. "I loved my parents. I don't know what to do without them."

"No, reckon you don't. You're a chicken-livered kid in some ways. Other ways you're a damned fool. Take hollering at Ackerman the way you done and trying to get your rifle out to shoot Malone. He'd have plugged you right in the guts if I hadn't had my gun on him. You know that?"

"Yeah." Mark swallowed. "I guess I wasn't thinking. When I heard his voice . . ."

"Oh, hell." Curtis squatted at the fire, his back to Mark. "Nobody can identify a voice. It ain't like seeing a man."

Mark was silent then. It wasn't a thing he could argue about. Maybe Curtis was right. Hearing a voice wasn't like seeing a man's face, and that was a fact. All he'd heard was one sentence of three words: *I found it.*

No, it sure wasn't like seeing a face: the color of a man's eyes, the length of his nose, his mouth, all definite things you could see and identify. But a voice that had said just three words. . . . No, Curtis was right. Now that Mark thought about it, he knew he couldn't be sure. Not sure enough to go into court and swear that Red Malone was the man who had murdered his parents.

Mark walked to the river and, hunkering down beside it, idly tossed rocks into a deep pool in front of him. It was a slow and turgid stream, entirely unlike the cold, swift-flowing Deschutes. More like the lower end of the Santiam before it ran into the Willamette.

Suddenly he was filled with a depressing sense of uncertainty. He couldn't live off the country the way Bronco Curtis could. Now he couldn't even go back to Prineville and get a haying job. Not after he'd run away. Ackerman might think he'd killed his folks. He asked himself why he'd left with Curtis the way he had, but he had no answer. He had acted without thinking, just as he had when he'd heard Malone's voice and grabbed for the rifle.

"Come and get it!" Curtis called.

Mark returned to the fire. He squatted beside it and ate his supper while dusk settled down; the rimrock and buttes to the west became vague and indistinct shapes as purple shadow flowed across the land. Then dusk turned to night, and for a time there was no sound but the whisper of a riffle just above them where the shallow water flowed over a gravel bed.

Curtis threw wood on the fire, then stretched out on the grass, his head on his saddle. As he rolled a cigarette, he said: "Well, I never figgered I'd be nursing a wet-nosed kid, but looks like that's what I'll be doing."

Angry, Mark said: "I didn't ask you to. I'll make out."

Curtis laughed. "The hell you will. You'd strike out across the high desert and die of thirst. Or some sand lizard would pull you out of the saddle and eat you alive."

It was ridicule, bitter and scathing, designed to take the hide off Mark's back and make him forget his grief. For a moment it succeeded. He said: "To hell with you. I'm not scared."

Curtis laughed again, turning his face so that the fire threw a dancing light upon it. Mark had not realized until that moment that Curtis's nose was long and hooked like a hawk's beak, that his dark face had a predatory cast to it.

"That's better," Curtis said. "You've got a little spunk in you. Mostly the Willamette Valley raises people like it does grass and ferns. Soft as mush. Too much moisture over there. Come winter, there's no strength to the grass. Over here the bunchgrass is like good rich hay, cured with all the strength in it."

"You don't owe me anything," Mark said. "I don't owe you anything, either. In the morning you ride one way, and I'll ride the other."

Curtis shook his head. "We'll stick together. For a while, anyhow. Maybe I can make something out of you."

"Why?" Mark demanded. "Why do you bother with me?"

Curtis stared at the flames, silent for several seconds. Then he said: "I can't forget the way I found you, lying beside the road and looking like hell wouldn't have you. Somebody's got to look after you, and I reckon that somebody's me."

"That's not good enough," Mark said. "You could have unloaded me in Prineville."

Curtis sat up and tossed his cigarette stub into the fire. "Yeah, there is something else. When I was a kid, younger'n you by a hell of a lot, I was in the same boat. I had to scratch or die, and, by God, I'd have died if a man hadn't come along and looked out for me. Let's say I'm paying that man back."

He grinned at Mark. "Hell, this kind of gab ain't getting us nowhere. Now, there's a thing or two about me you'd better know. I'm a getting man. When I see what I want, I'll take it. I've got some money. Been saving for quite a spell, then got into a poker game a week or so ago and hit it lucky. That's why I'm here. I always have liked it on this side of the mountains. I don't have much more'n a nest egg, but before I'm done, I'll hatch it into the biggest damned ranch in eastern Oregon."

He leaned forward, his knees under his chin. "That was why I was arguing with Red. We busted up this morning, and he figgered I'd show in Prineville, so he was waiting for me. He wanted to go to The Dalles. It's a river town with a lot of crooked gamblers and pimps and women who'll do anything you ask 'em if you pay 'em, and suckers waiting to be taken. But that's Red's kind of life. It ain't mine."

He laughed, a dry, humorless sound. "Red wanted me to go because he needed my money, but I didn't figger that way. He'll wind up with a slug in him or stretching rope, but me, I aim to get me a ranch, and I'll keep looking till I find what I want. I'm just as tough as the country. Now we're gonna find out if you are, or whether you're as soft as that Willamette Valley grass. But don't make no more mistakes like you done with Red. If a man's on the shoot, accommodate him."

Mark nodded as if he understood, but he didn't, not really. He wondered what would have happened if his folks had lived and bought the ranch on the Ochoco. They were kindly people, who had taught him about God and law and being neighborly. Probably they should have stayed in the Willamette Valley, for that was their kind of country.

He thought of the damp kiss of the wind that blew in from the Pacific, the ferns that were tall and green and utterly useless, and the grass that lost its strength in winter just as Curtis said. No, it wasn't Bronco Curtis's country, but it had been his.

He stared at the fire, vaguely aware of the coyote chorus that broke out from a distant rim to the south, and he wondered if he could change, if he could learn from Curtis all that he had to know. At least the man had left the door open, and he would go with him, and try.

They headed south the next morning, traveling across the high desert with its naked rims and juniper forest and sagebrush, and bunchgrass in spots as high as a man's stirrups. Good stock country, Bronco said, or would be if there was water. He seemed to be in no hurry, and apparently he wasn't headed anywhere in particular.

They angled back and forth, toward the pines in the foothills of the Cascades, or again into the desert. Sometimes they made a dry camp; sometimes they found water. Occasionally they put up at a ranch, with Bronco looking everything over and asking questions, and often turning down offers of a job. They crossed the line into California, and then into Nevada.

Every day Mark learned something. From observation, from the things Bronco said, from having to do things he had never done before. He learned to ride, and, as Bronco had told him in Prineville, he found that in time he lost his soreness, that he could stay in the saddle day after day.

He lost count of those days as they dropped behind, and eventually time blunted his grief. When he thought about what had happened on the Deschutes that bitter night, it seemed to him it was in the dim past, a past he had to forget because it was too painful to remember.

When Bronco decided Mark would do, he had him get his revolver out of the slicker. He taught the boy how to wear it, how to draw, and he gave grudging praise as Mark improved. When they hit a town, they bought large quantities of ammunition. At first Mark paid for them, but his money was soon gone, and after that Bronco bought them. Every night, if they were camped by themselves, Bronco had Mark practice.

They became friends of a sort, with Bronco giving the orders, a relationship that Mark accepted because he had no choice. He was never sure what was in the other man's mind, and he knew better than to ask, but he didn't doubt that Bronco Curtis had a definite purpose. He was that kind of man.

But Mark had a purpose, too, and he was accomplishing it, learning to live off the country. Sometimes at night when he couldn't sleep, he would think about the murder of his parents, and he would promise himself that someday he would go back and put the stone markers on the graves, as Fred Baxes had suggested, and then he'd start out on the trail of the murderer.

Always on the following day, when he was in the saddle, his resolve would melt as he examined it in daylight. The trail was too cold, the man was long gone, and only the foolish devoted their lives to the grim purpose of revenge. He had his own future, his own life, and even under the tough tutorship of Bronco Curtis he never entirely lost what his folks had taught him, principles about God and man and law.

He grew taller and he lost weight. Peach fuzz sprouted on his face, and black whiskers grew on Bronco's. Both wore their guns; they were always careful with strangers, never giving them the bulge. When they rode into town and stood together at a bar or bought supplies and ammunition in a store, people let them alone, giving them the respect they would have given a pair of wolves that had drifted into town from the wilderness.

Eventually it occurred to Mark that they had a wolf look about them, maybe a wolf smell. Bronco laughed when Mark mentioned it to him. "You're damned right we have. If we looked and acted like we was soft, people would jump us same as a pack of dogs jump a stray that gets into the wrong neighborhood. But if you look and act like you're tough, by God, they'll let you alone. You might be a hardcase like you look, and there ain't many men who are real anxious to find out."

He gave Mark a long, measuring look. "We've been lucky we ain't run into somebody who did want to find out. If we keep riding, we will. Maybe some drunk. Or some son-of-a-bitch who wants to fight just for the hell of it. If that happens, you watch my back. I can take care of the man in front of me, but I sure can't keep my eyes on the one behind me. If it's in a saloon, cover the bartender. Some of 'em won't butt in no matter what. Other ones will. When they do, it's on the side of the man they know."

Mark listened and nodded, not thinking anything of the sort would happen. But it did the next day. They hit a small place in Nevada just north of Quinn River, a couple of houses and a store and saloon in one false-fronted building. A lathered horse was tied in front of the building, but no one was inside except a skinny man who stood fidgeting behind the bar.

"Watch it, boy," Bronco said in a low tone. "Something wrong here."

The bar consisted of two unplaned planks set on barrels. There was no mirror in the place, no fancy chandelier suspended from the ceiling, no brass foot rail. A shelf behind the skinny man held a dozen or more bottles and some glasses, most of them dirty.

"What'll it be, gents?" the skinny man asked, grinning nervously.

Bronco glanced around the room, then turned his gaze to the skinny man. "Who's here?"

"Nobody."

Bronco motioned to the lathered horse. "I reckon that animal walked up and tied himself."

"Oh, that." The skinny man shrugged. "A cowboy rode up a while ago. He's out back."

"Let's ride, Mark," Bronco said.

"How about your drink?" the skinny man asked.

Bronco didn't answer. He took two steps toward the door, then wheeled as a man came in through the back, calling: "Freeze, mister. I'm swapping horses."

The newcomer was pulling his gun as he said it. Bronco didn't take time to ask questions. He went for his gun, and even though the other man had his revolver almost clear of leather, he never got off a shot. Bronco was that much faster. His bullet caught the man in the belly.

For a moment Mark was shocked by surprise at the suddenness of the whole thing. Then he remembered what Bronco had told him, and he drew his gun just as the skinny man was straightening up, a sawed-off shotgun in his hands. He stared at Mark, blinking, and laid the shotgun on the bar as Bronco wheeled to face him.

"You're lucky to be alive, mister," Bronco said.

"I didn't mean nothing." The skinny man's face had turned green, and sweat was rolling down his cheeks and on down his chin. "I just don't like my place shot all to hell."

"Get out here," Bronco said, and holstered his gun. "Keep him covered, Mark. If he makes a fast move, shoot him in the guts."

The skinny man walked around the end of the bar, feet dragging, gazing at Mark as if uncertain how long he had to live. Bronco ran his hands down the front of the man, down his sides, then grabbed a shoulder and yanked him around and felt of his back.

"Outside," Bronco said, giving the fellow a push toward the door. "Put up your gun, Mark. We'll be moseying. This jasper is taking a walk in front of us."

"I told you I didn't mean nothing," the skinny man whined.

"Shut up," Bronco said in disgust. "You're lying like hell. You figured the boy here would stand pat and you'd let me have it in the back, then plug the boy and rob us. And the booger who wanted to swap horses. You had one carcass to bury, so you figured you'd just dig the grave three times as wide. Now get outside."

The skinny man obeyed. Mark and Bronco mounted and turned north. The bartender walked in front of them for fifty yards. Bronco let him go back, saying: "I'll put a window in your skull if you're here the next time I ride through. Now git."

He started back in a shambling run. Bronco lifted his horse into a gallop, Mark matching the pace. For a time Mark thought he was going to be sick. He had never seen a man shot down before; he hadn't looked at the body, but it was enough to know it was there. But what bothered him most was the way Bronco took it, as if killing a man was all part of the day's work.

Presently Bronco pulled his horse down to a slower pace. Before dark they crossed back into Oregon. That night after supper Mark asked: "How'd you catch on so quick?"

Bronco grinned. "I've been on the dodge a time or two. You get so you smell things like that. My guess was that the booger I plugged had a posse on his tail and needed a fresh horse bad. He probably hadn't been there long. He may have been hooked up with the skinny gent, but then again maybe he wasn't. You never know about a deal like that, and you can't wait to find out."

Bronco didn't commend Mark for his quick thinking, but Mark didn't expect him to. He knew Bronco too well. Now he knew him a little better yet. The incident had taught him two things: Bronco had been wanted by the law, and Bronco could kill a man and take it in stride.

Both facts worried him for a time. They reminded him of a remark Bud Ackerman had made in Prineville, about its being funny Bronco had showed up so quickly after Mark had discovered the murder of his parents. Then Mark reminded himself that Bronco hadn't been the man he'd caught getting out of the wagon. Besides, the kind of murderer who would knife two sleeping people wouldn't be bothering with a boy like Mark. The suspicion died.

In the morning they rode northwest. Mark wondered how long this aimless wandering would last, but he didn't ask. He was afraid to do or say anything that might give Bronco an excuse to tell Mark to go his own way. He wasn't sure Bronco wanted such an excuse, but he might. The shooting had demonstrated more than anything else that had happened how raw and violent this country was. Mark knew he had graduated out of the greenhorn class, but he also knew he was a long way from being able to take care of himself.

Near the end of the week they reached an alkali-crusted lake, the shore around it the most sterile piece of ground Mark had ever seen. It was, Bronco said: "Coyote country with a coyote smell about it."

Even in late summer the wind was bitter cold. A human skull lay at the edge of the water, grinning at them as they rode past. Mark shivered in spite of himself, and he was glad to get out of the valley. As they picked their way through a break in the rimrock to the north, Mark was convinced that the ghost of the man whose skull they had seen was still in the valley.

He asked Bronco if he knew what the place was called. When Bronco answered—"Ghost Valley."—Mark knew he was right. He felt it in the back of his neck and along his spine and deep down in his belly.

"Ever been here before?" Mark asked.

"No, but I've heard about it," Bronco answered. "'Most everybody circles it, but hell, I figger you ain't got nothing to worry about if the ghost is there but the man ain't."

Late in the afternoon they reached a combination store and saloon set alongside a trail that ran south to Nevada. There was a water hole nearby, the only sweet water for miles around. Bronco said: "Someday men will die for that water, but it ain't worth a killing to me. We'll do better."

They went inside, and Bronco bought two cans of peaches. They opened the cans with their pocket knives, drank the juice, and speared the peaches with their knife blades and ate them. Then Bronco began asking about the country and the people who came past and the ranches to the east he'd heard about.

"Big outfits," the man said. "Yonder is Sherman Valley. Bearpaw is on this side of the valley, and Rocking Chair is on the other side at the foot of Shadow Mountain. Funny thing. The Triangle R is east of Shadow Mountain, not more'n six or eight miles the way the crow flies, but damned if they don't have to go fifty if they want to visit. You don't climb Shadow Mountain less'n you're a mountain goat."

Bronco wiped the peach juice off his face with his sleeve. "Good grass there, I reckon, or those outfits wouldn't be as big as you're claiming they are."

"Grass?" The man laughed. "Mister, the grass is so high they lose their cows in it. Fact." He shook his head. "I don't know why I stay in this damned desert. Sometimes I ride over there just to look at a country that's green grass and not gray green like it is here. This water hole's gonna be worth a fortune someday, but I may die of old age before it is."

The man scratched the back of his neck. "If I was a young feller like you boys, I'd have me a look over there. Them spreads can always use a couple of good buckaroos, if you're looking for jobs."

"Any little outfits?" Bronco asked.

"Sure. In the north end of the valley around the Army post. It's next to the Blue Mountains where they can get timber for cabins. Game's close. Good fishing they tell me in Doolin Creek. A lot of land just for the taking, or close to it. Swamp land, you know. A dollar and a quarter an acre to the state, and ten percent down. Not that it's really swamp land, you understand, but that's what they call it on the map, and the state's glad to get the money without looking at every acre."

Bronco acted as if he wasn't listening, but Mark, watching, knew he was. Bronco hadn't been sure what he was looking for, but he recognized it when he heard about it.

"Reckon we'll camp here tonight," Bronco said.

"Sure," the man said. "Two bits apiece for your horses. Water's free to people."

"Now that's generous as hell," Bronco said. "You mean folks pay you for water?"

"You're damned right," the man said. "Better'n riding another fifty miles, ain't it?"

Bronco paid him and walked out. That night he shaved for the first time in weeks. By way of explanation, he said: "Time I was getting the wolf look off my mug. In the morning we'll buy a couple of new shirts."

That, Mark thought, was Bronco's way of telling him the days of aimless riding were over.

Chapter Five

At noon the next day they stopped on the west rim of Sherman Valley. For a long time Bronco Curtis stood looking down into the valley as if he could not fill himself with the sight of it. For Mark, too, it was an impressive sight, utterly unlike the barren country through which they had been traveling.

A series of long, pine-covered ridges to the north would be the Blue Mountains, Mark thought, but he didn't know the name of the brown hills to the east, which tipped up to a high peak farther south. Mark remembered that the man at the water hole had mentioned Shadow Mountain.

From where Mark stood he could not see any ridges or rims marking the south end of the valley, but it was probably lost in distance. The west rim was a definite, meandering line, dropping one hundred feet or more from the sage-covered plateau to the almost level floor of the valley.

The lush green below them amazed Mark more than anything else. There was considerable sage, particularly around the edges where the land was rocky and dry. A few junipers, some patches of greasewood, and in the middle of the valley Mark could see two lakes, one probably draining into the other, which apparently had no outlet.

A twisting line of willows marked a creek that brawled down out of the Blue Mountains to take its meandering course across the valley to the first lake. The lower end of the creek and the area around the lakes seemed to be a vast swamp covered by cat-tails and tulles, but the great bulk of the valley, particularly the northern part on both sides of the creek, was covered by grass.

"By God," Bronco said in awe. "The old gent at the water hole was right when he said this was green-green. A cow heaven if I ever seen one. Even that swamp part wouldn't be so bad. Them tulles would give protection in bad weather. It's my guess a man wouldn't have to feed much unless a winter was awful bad."

"Ever been here before?" Mark asked.

"No, but I've heard about all this country," Bronco answered. "The stream's Doolin Creek. Goes into Paiute Lake and then drains into Sherman Lake. That bunch of buildings you see yonder." He pointed to where the creek broke out of the Blue Mountains. "That's Camp Sherman." He jammed his hands deep into his pants pockets. "Mark, there'll be a town down there in the valley someday and fifty ranches where there's one now. But there'll always be more cows than people."

"This what you're looking for?"

Bronco took his time answering. He teetered back and forth on his tall heels, then said: "No. Too much of it. If a man had a big herd and could hire a crew to fight and hold a chunk of the grass, he could make it stick. From what I've heard, there's just two big outfits in the valley. You can't see either one of 'em from here, but Rocking Chair must be over yonder at the foot of Shadow Mountain, and Bearpaw's probably straight south from where we're standing. There's sure a hell of a lot more grass in the valley than them two spreads need, but if you 'n' me moved in with a shirt tailful of cows, we'd get shot right between the eyes."

Bronco turned to his horse. "Let's ride. If we keep looking, we'll find something our size."

He mounted and took the road, which dropped to the valley through a break in the rimrock. Mark, catching up with him when they reached the bottom, glanced at Bronco's face, more alive and eager than he had ever seen it.

WAYNE D. OVERHOLSER

Bronco was envious of the men who owned Rocking Chair and Bearpaw, Mark thought, probably wishing he had come to Sherman Valley five years ago with a herd of California cattle and a crew and claimed the grass as they had done. Bronco was tough and practical, but he had his dreams, too, and Mark would have given odds that within five years he'd turn some of his dreams into reality.

They rode in silence, Bronco taking in every detail of the scene before him. One thing he had said back up on the rim stayed in Mark's mind. "If you 'n' me moved in with a shirt tailful of cows, we'd get shot right between the eyes." *You 'n' me.* He had never said it quite that way before.

Mark had assumed that sooner or later Bronco would get tired of doing what he had once called "nursing a wet-nosed kid." Mark had been afraid to look forward to the time when Bronco would tell him they were finished, as he had told Red Malone back there in Prineville, afraid to think what he would do then.

But Mark hadn't worried about it. The summer had given him a confidence he had lacked. He knew he wouldn't starve. Now he realized Bronco didn't intend for them to break up, that he was including Mark in the dream that had been taking shape through all these weeks.

At first Mark was relieved. Bronco would look out for him through the winter just as he had all summer. Bronco had said it as if there was no doubt in his mind about Mark's staying with him, as if theirs was a partnership that would go on indefinitely. Then he began asking himself why, and he could not think of an answer that made sense.

Bronco was by nature a lone wolf, and Mark had no illusions about any affection that the man had for him. Friendship, perhaps, but one which could continue only on the basis that it had in the past, with Bronco giving the orders and Mark accepting them without argument. Mark was surprised at the sudden

37

rebellion that took possession of him, and the resentment that it created. He had no right to feel that way, and he was ashamed of it.

He owed Bronco plenty, including his life in Prineville, when Red Malone would have killed him. Maybe it was a simple matter of working for Bronco, of having a job and a place to live and something to eat, and then, thinking of it that way, he got over the resentment. At least he would stay with Bronco through the winter.

They left the road where it turned north toward Camp Sherman; splashed across Doolin Creek, a languid stream that hardly seemed to move over the muddy bottom; rammed their way through the willow jungle on the east side; and came out on the grass. They angled northeast, and late in the afternoon they reached the road. They were in the sagebrush again, the steep, brown hills directly in front of them.

Bronco had given no hint of where he was headed, and Mark, with the sun resting atop the rim behind them, began to wonder. He asked: "Are we going to Idaho?"

An unexpected grin eased the severity of expression on Bronco's dark face. "I reckon we would if we kept going." He nodded at a set of buildings north of the road. "Maybe they've got supper on the stove. Let's find out."

They left the road to follow the wheel ruts that led to the ranch, climbing now, for the buildings were set on a bench beside a small stream, the hills rising directly behind the ranch. A dozen pines were scattered on both sides of the creek, two of them in front of the house and close enough to shade it through most of the day.

It was a pleasant place, clean and orderly, and Mark, glancing at the outbuildings and corrals, had a feeling that people lived here because they liked it and not because they had become so tired they couldn't keep going, which seemed to be true of many greasy-sack spreads he had seen during the summer. This was a ranch site a man would pick because he was the first one here and so had his choice.

Suddenly a wild and unreasoning fear possessed Mark. Bronco might decide this was the place he wanted, and, if he did, he'd get it, one way or the other. Mark had never forgotten what Bronco had said that night when they were camped on Crooked River. "I'm a getting man. When I see what I want, I'll take it." Since then nothing had happened to make Mark think he hadn't meant what he'd said.

The barn and the outbuildings were made of lumber, but the house was log, tall and square and well-built. Grass ran up to the front door. Here there was no white-crusted bare spot where the wash water was thrown. Instead, there was a row of red geraniums set close to the house and a climber rose at the corner, which had probably been given life through the summer by the rinse water.

A man had been washing on the back porch. Now he walked toward Bronco and Mark, who had reined up in front of the house, his hair damp and carefully combed in a high roach above his forehead. He said—"Good evening."—in a neutral voice, his gaze switching from Bronco to Mark and back again.

Bronco said—"Howdy."—and Mark nodded. Both waited for the man to make up his mind, Mark thinking it was a good thing they had bought new shirts and Bronco had shaved last night.

The man was thirty-five or more, Mark guessed, quite tall and slightly stooped and smooth-shaven, a spare, gray man who wore steel-rimmed spectacles. He was no fire-eater, Mark thought, and was vaguely disappointed. To him this fellow looked more like a Willamette Valley farmer than an eastern Oregon rancher.

"Light and rest your saddles," the man said after he had given them a careful scrutiny. "I'll have my daughter fry some extra meat. We're having antelope steak."

"Thank you kindly," Bronco said, and turned toward the corral, Mark following.

When they returned to the house, the man met them and held out his hand. "I'm Herb Jackson," he said. "This is the Circle J."

"Bronco Curtis," Bronco said as he shook hands. "My partner, Mark Kelton."

"Pleased to meet you," Jackson said, giving Mark's hand a firm shake, his gaze so direct it was embarrassing. Then he motioned toward the pump. "Wash up if you care to. I'll go in and give my daughter a hand."

He disappeared into the kitchen. Bronco pumped a wash pan of water, scrubbed briskly, and dried. As Mark washed, Bronco said: "We're getting close. Real close."

Mark dried, thinking he had been afraid of this very thing. Bronco had neither the patience nor the vision to build something from scratch. Instead, he would take what another man had built and go on from there.

Mark walked to the corner of the house and looked out toward the valley. Dark shadow covered the western half of the valley, the sun still sharp and bright on the eastern hills.

Jackson didn't wear a gun. He didn't look the least part of a fighting man. The question that had been half formulated in Mark's mind earlier in the afternoon now began to nag him. What would he do if Bronco tried to coerce Jackson into selling?

Mark would profit if Bronco succeeded. He was Bronco's partner. He'd have a place to live, a place to work, a roof over his head and a good tight one, too, by the look of the outside of the house. Then another question hit Mark. What chance would he, an eighteen-year-old boy, have against a tough hand like Bronco Curtis? None. It would be like stepping on a fat ant.

Jackson called from the door: "Come and get it!"

Mark followed Bronco into the house. Jackson introduced them to his daughter Ruth. She was probably seventeen, Mark guessed, a pretty girl with blue-black hair, dark brown eyes set in an oval face, and an impertinent nose. When she gave Mark her small brown hand, her grip was as firm as her father's, her gaze as direct. She was suspicious of them, Mark thought, but she wasn't afraid, and it struck him that he had no cause to worry about the Jacksons. It would not be easy to take anything from them they didn't want to give.

Jackson led the way to the table that was set for four. As Mark sat down, he was haunted by a feeling that this kitchen was little different from what his mother's had been in the Willamette Valley: white curtains at the two windows, the big range, the pantry door, which was open, the cherry-wood sideboard set against the opposite wall with a number of colored dishes placed upright against the back.

As Mark pulled up his chair, Jackson bowed his head. He said: "We thank Thee, Lord, for this day and for this food and for the bountiful blessings Thou hast bestowed upon us. Amen."

Mark had to turn his face to hide a grin. Bronco had started to reach for the platter of meat when Jackson began the blessing. He had been shocked into immobility, his hand suspended in mid-air. Now he withdrew it, his face turning brick-red. It was probably the first time he had ever sat down at a table where someone said a blessing.

"Help yourself to the meat, Mister Curtis," Jackson said. "There is one good thing about this country. We have ample game. Antelope. Deer. Sage hen. Ducks and geese in season." He nodded at Ruth. "With a good cook it's manna in the wilderness."

Ruth blushed and looked away, embarrassed. Bronco needed no more urging. He helped himself liberally and began eating in his usual noisy fashion. Mark covertly watched Ruth. He had gone to school with girls his age and played with them, but that seemed a long time ago. He had seen few women during the summer, and no girls at all except the little ones with pigtails who hid behind their mothers' skirts.

It was a pleasure to sit and look at Ruth. If she was aware of his scrutiny, she ignored it. Her front teeth were small and white, her cheek bones were rather high, her lips long and full. The skin of her face, deeply tanned, had a fine texture.

She could ride well, Mark guessed, and probably helped her father with the cattle. She was still a girl, her breasts quite small under the blouse of her calico dress, but in time she would be a fine-looking woman, Mark thought, and was a little surprised at the line his thinking took.

When Bronco finished eating, he sat back and belched as usual, then wiped his sleeve across his mouth. "Me and Mark here are looking for a place to settle down," he said. "Anything for sale hereabouts?"

Jackson nodded. "A man named Orry Andrews owns the Cross Seven on the other side of the Paradise Hills. It's in Ten Mile Valley, good grass and plenty of hay land. The winters are more severe there than here, but not too cold."

"We'll have a look in the morning," Bronco said.

"You might find a place for sale in Sherman Valley," Jackson said. "A few people are talking about moving, with the Indians as uneasy as they are. Personally I don't think we have anything to worry about with the military here, although I have to admit they don't keep enough soldiers at Camp Sherman to do any good if there was an uprising."

"Some folks scare easy," Bronco said.

"That's true," Jackson agreed. "If you decide to look around in Sherman Valley, I have one piece of advice. Stay in the north. There are two big ranches that claim most of the grass, Rocking Chair and Bearpaw. Dave Nolan owns Rocking Chair. Bearpaw belongs to Matt Ardell. The two men are entirely different, but alike in the sense that they act as if the Lord gave them the earth and all that is upon it."

The bitterness in his voice amused Bronco. He said: "Well, one way to beat a big man is to be bigger." He rose. "I think we'll roll in. We've come a ways today."

"Have breakfast with us in the morning," Jackson said.

"Be glad to," Bronco said, and left the house.

Mark paused beside Ruth's chair. He said: "Thank you for the meal."

She glanced at him shyly. "You're welcome," she said, and looked away again.

When Mark was outside, Bronco said: "She's a right purty heifer. I reckon she's worth your staying around here for."

Mark glanced at him, embarrassed, not sure how Bronco meant it, but the big man was looking straight ahead, his mind on other things. Then Mark, his thoughts turning to Ruth again, knew that he did want to stay here, wanted to more than he had ever wanted anything in his life.

Chapter Six

As long as Mark lived, he would never forget his first sight of Ten Mile Valley. He and Bronco reached the summit of the Paradise Hills an hour after they left the Circle J. The sun, barely above the rim to the east, had turned the sky gold and scarlet. A breeze touched the sage below them so the valley looked like a great silver sea threaded by the green of the willows that grew along the creek.

Two forks of the stream came together directly below the ridge where Mark and Bronco sat their saddles. From what Herb Jackson had told them, the creek would be Ten Mile, not a large stream so late in the summer, but at this altitude there would likely be a heavy snowfall, and, when it went off in late spring or early summer, the creek would carry ample water for irrigation.

Mark guessed the valley was four or five miles wide, the hills to the north covered by pines, the rim on the south a sheer, raked wall with only a few breaks. The ridges to the east were much like the Paradise Hills, where Mark was now, except that the creek had cut an opening through them, which looked like a narrow crack at this distance.

Bronco had called Sherman Valley a cow heaven. This was exactly the same in miniature, with the exception of a few patches of greasewood and what seemed to be a considerable patch of swamp in the low end of the valley. Then Mark remembered that even the tulles had their use.

Mark glanced at Bronco's face. The man sat his saddle as if he were frozen, one hand folded over the horn. The predatory expression that often marked his face was completely gone. In its place was one of beatific peace, as if he had told God what he wanted and God had created it for him. But the thought remained unvoiced in Mark's mind. Bronco would have laughed if Mark had expressed it, for Bronco Curtis was not one to give God credit.

Bronco nodded at Mark, smiling. "We ain't looking any more. We're gonna own this valley."

Bronco touched up his horse and rode down the rocky slope through the scattered junipers. Mark followed, saying nothing, not wanting to break the spell that had been cast upon Bronco. He was remembering how Bronco had said: "We're gonna own this valley."

So he was included in whatever plans Bronco had. It troubled him just as he had been troubled when they'd first seen Jackson's Circle J the day before. There was a quality about Bronco that frightened Mark, a sort of leashed strength that, once turned loose, would crush anything or anybody who stood in his way, a driving will that would not be hampered by moral scruples. Mark didn't know what Bronco planned to do, but whatever it was, Mark would be a part of it. The trouble was he had no choice. Bronco simply wouldn't give him a choice.

They crossed a dry bench, scaring up a couple of sage hens as they rode. A little later an antelope bounded off to the south. Bronco turned to Mark, grinning. "Jackson was right. A man could take a big chunk of his living right out of the country."

Later they swung down to the creek, the sun cutting away the night chill. A number of Cross Seven cows and calves were in the willows beside the stream. Noticing them, Mark asked: "How big a herd does Andrews own?"

"Jackson didn't say," Bronco answered, "but it ain't big enough, not near big enough for us."

In midmorning they crossed a hay meadow and came to the Cross Seven buildings. They were poor and run-down compared to Jackson's Circle J: a slab shed for a barn, a couple of pole corrals with three horses in the one next to the barn, an outhouse, and a log cabin with a dirt roof.

There were a number of haystacks in the meadow, several of them looking as if they had been carried over for a couple of seasons. Even so, there wasn't enough hay to take any sizeable herd through a rough winter.

A man who had been mending a bridle in front of the shed came toward them. Bronco stepped down without an invitation, motioning for Mark to do the same. When the man reached them, Bronco held out his hand. "I'm Bronco Curtis." He nodded at Mark. "My partner, Mark Kelton."

"I'm Orry Andrews," the man said as he shook hands. "Glad to see you. Gets a mite lonesome here. Not many strangers ride through this country."

Andrews was a small man with pale eyes and a ragged beard on his chin, the rest of his face smooth-shaven. He was about sixty, Mark guessed, although he looked older. Again Mark had a vague feeling of disappointment just as he had when he'd seen Fred Baxes and Bud Ackerman.

Mark's notion that it took a tough breed of men to survive in eastern Oregon had been jolted a good many times during the summer. There was nothing tough in Orry Andrews's appearance, and he wasn't likely to survive, either. Bronco's eyes were giving him a rough going-over, and he seemed to shrink in size before Bronco's gaze.

"Come on in," Andrews said. "I got up late this morning. I reckon the coffee's still warm."

"No." Bronco shoved his big hands under his belt and, rocking back on his heels, looked as formidable as Mark had ever seen him. "Herb Jackson said your outfit was for sale. We'll buy you out."

Just like that. "We'll buy you out." No preliminaries, no negotiating, no haggling. Andrews scratched a cheek, his hands heavy-jointed. Mark felt sympathy for him. He had seen men like him in the Willamette Valley who had worked hard all their lives but still never got ahead.

Now he saw hope brighten the man's face, but there was suspicion there, too, as if he feared this was too good to be true. Or perhaps he was afraid of Bronco. He had cause to be, Mark thought as he glanced at Bronco's dark face, and suddenly he realized a great weight was pressing against his chest and he was having trouble breathing.

"Yeah, the place is for sale," Andrews said. "I've got title to a section of swamp land. I own three horses you see in the corral and more'n two hundred head of cattle, most of 'em cows that'll calve next spring. I ain't sure, but I guess I've got about thirty steers ready to market."

He nodded toward the mountains. "They're back in the timber with most of my stock. You just seen a few cows and calves on the creek as you rode in. I was fixing to start gathering tomorrow. I drive my steers to the railroad with the Triangle R herd."

Andrews motioned south. "It's a big outfit about thirty miles from here. They always let me go along. You know, swapping my help on the drive for the privilege of throwing my little jag of steers in with their herd."

Bronco listened impatiently. Now he asked brusquely: "What's your price?"

"Five thousand dollars."

Bronco laughed at him. "You're high, Andrews. Sitting out here by yourself, you're a sitting duck for some bunch of Paiutes that take a notion to have a little fun. You'll lose your hair one of these mornings."

Andrews shrugged. "I ain't worried about that, Mister Curtis. The Paiutes ain't ornery. Old Winnemucca is a friendly booger, and he's their chief."

"No old chief is going to keep the young bucks in line," Bronco said. "Not if they get to feeling foxy. I'll give you $1,000." He motioned to the corral. "And you can take your pick of the horses and anything you need out of the house."

"Oh, I'd just take a few clothes and enough grub to last me till I get to Camp Sherman. And my Henry rifle." He shook his head. "But I couldn't take a thousand. I don't have to sell, you know. The only reason I figgered to was because the winters are getting a mite hard on my joints. I aim to live on the Rogue. Winters are purty mild there, I heard."

Bronco put a hand on the butt of his gun. He said: "Friend, I'm going to have your spread. I'll split the difference with you. If you're smart, you'll take it."

Andrews dragged a scuffed boot toe through the dust. He said: "I just brought in a wagon load of supplies. There's a store close to Camp Sherman, and I fetched in enough to last me all winter. I figgered that if I sold, I'd throw in . . ."

"Three thousand dollars," Bronco said, "and you'll throw the supplies in."

Andrews sighed. "All right, it's a deal. I guess you'll want some papers made out." He stopped. "Got the money on you?"

"Sure it's on me." Bronco nodded at Mark. "Stay here."

He strode toward the cabin, Mark's gaze following him. He wondered why Bronco had told him to stay here. Maybe he intended to browbeat Andrews down to his original offer of $1,000. At a time like this there was no yielding in Bronco Curtis. If there was any giving to be done, it would come from Orry Andrews.

Leaving his sorrel ground-hitched, Mark walked to the corral. A buckskin gelding looked like a fair saddle horse. The two bay mares were skinny, but maybe they'd do hitched to a mowing machine or a wagon.

He glanced into the shed. The stable side needed cleaning out. The other side was a mess, harness and a couple of saddles and odds and ends that Andrews had gathered since the day he'd put up the building.

Mark hunkered in the shade of the shed, wondering how much money Bronco had. He'd never said, but Mark judged it wasn't much over the $3,000 he'd offered Andrews. He asked himself how Bronco aimed to get ahead. Right now the Cross Seven was a long way from being the dream ranch Bronco wanted. A beginning, but a pretty sorry one.

They came out of the cabin, a partly filled sack under Andrews's right arm, a Henry rifle in his left hand. He didn't look particularly unhappy, so he'd probably got his $3,000. He saddled the buckskin, Bronco stopping beside Mark long enough to say: "I'm going with him so he can tell me something about the range. Clean the cabin up. It's a mess."

Mark waited until they rode off, going upstream, then he put his sorrel into the corral with the mares and went into the cabin. It had a rough board floor, but, aside from that, it was as dirty and smelled as bad as the Baxes' cabin. He built up the fire, brought water from the creek, heated it, and started to clean up.

By evening the cabin smelled and looked better. It seemed bigger, as if Mark had added a few feet on all sides. Mark had carried out armload after armload of junk. Now there was a pile of litter in front that would have to be hauled off in the wagon. Apparently Orry Andrews was a man who couldn't throw a tin can away.

Bronco did not return until dusk. Mark had supper ready and had taken the bedding outside to air. "You've been working, looks like," Bronco said approvingly, then he gave Mark a resounding slap on the back. "Partner, we've got ourselves a spread. With the summer range in the mountains and the hay a man can raise along the creek, we'll have a layout that'll match the Triangle R or any of the rest of 'em."

Mark had never seen Bronco as exuberant as he was after supper. He lolled on the bed as Mark washed dishes, talking excitedly about the future and always bringing Mark in as if the outfit would be half his.

"We've got to lay in more grub and a hell of a lot more ammunition," Bronco said, "in case them Paiutes do get boogery. Andrews showed me a wagon road over the Paradise Hills. Ain't much, but we'll get a wagon over it all right. Andrews says there's a sawmill north of the fort. Come spring, we'll haul lumber in and build a house. A big house, by God. I'll find a woman, too." He laughed. "Man needs a woman."

"Nobody's going to get rich very fast with two hundred head of cattle," Mark said.

"You think we're gonna sit pat with two hundred head?" Bronco asked. "Why, hell, there's no end to what we can do with this valley long as we control all of it. It won't be two hundred head. It'll be two thousand. Maybe more. We'll put up a barn. A bunkhouse. A cook shack. Mark, all of a sudden I feel like a colt turned into grass up to his belly. We'll have to work, but we can do it."

Mark went on washing dishes, saying nothing, but he couldn't keep from wondering where the money was coming from. Bronco was not a man to dream without having some idea of how he was going to work the dream out, but it was incredible to Mark that he had the kind of money he'd need to do everything he was talking about.

Bronco got up and yawned. "I forgot to tell you. I'm riding south to the Triangle R to see about driving our steers to Winnemucca. When I come back, we'll start rounding 'em up. Gonna be a job for the two of us 'cause they ain't started down out of the mountains yet. I'll be gone two, three days. You can find plenty to do. Get some wood in if you run out of chores. I don't want to get cold this winter."

Bronco left the next morning, still intoxicated from his dream that had grown bigger during the night. He had not returned two days later when Herb Jackson rode in. When he saw Mark, his first question was: "Where's Orry Andrews?"

"Sold out to Bronco Curtis the morning after we left your place," Mark said. "He left the same day. Didn't take anything but his buckskin, his Henry rifle, and some clothes."

Jackson's face turned gray. "Where's Curtis?"

"Went to the Triangle R to see about driving our steers south with their herd. Andrews said there was about thirty ready to go. Get down, Mister Jackson, and set a while."

Jackson shook his head. "I can't stay. Looks like I've got work to do. Which way did Orry go when he left?"

"Up the creek."

"Alone?"

"No, Bronco went with him. Wanted Andrews to tell him all he could about the range, he said."

Jackson's lips squeezed together so tightly they pursed out on both sides and turned white. He reached up and shifted his glasses higher on his nose. Then he said in a low tone: "Orry Andrews would never leave this country without telling me and Ruth good bye. Think that over, boy. Think it over carefully."

He wheeled his horse and rode away. Mark, staring after him, thought about what Jackson had implied without actually saying it, and instantly built a defense for Bronco in his mind. Bronco Curtis was a tough, unyielding man, a man to be feared, a getting man by his own admission. "But he's not a murderer, not a cold-blooded murderer." Only after the words had come out of his mouth did Mark realize he had said them aloud, shouting them at Jackson, who was too far away to hear, but he shouted again: "He wouldn't kill a man for $3,000."

Then he was silent, a little sick as he wondered what Bronco would do when he heard what Jackson had said.

Chapter Seven

B ronco returned late the day after Herb Jackson's visit. He
said: "Mark, that Triangle R is some outfit. A big stone
house, stockade corrals, the biggest damned barn you ever seen,
and the finest horses I ever laid eyes on. This John Runyan's a
man who sure knows how to enjoy hisself. Dresses and acts like
a Spanish *don*. Some of his fancy California friends were visit-
ing, so they had horse races every day I was there. They were
betting like fools. Why, I seen as much as $1,000 change hands
on one race."

He led his horse into the stable and rubbed him down. "Glad
you got things cleaned up around here. Andrews was a lazy
booger." He glanced at Mark. "Get along all right?"

"Sure," Mark said.

"In a couple of weeks we'll start our gather. I'll go with the
Triangle R drive. Runyan's a real neighborly gent. Says he's got
a couple of carpenters he'll send me next summer and they can
build our house. Come spring, I'll buy two, three hundred head
of cows and some good bulls. We'll get another work team and a
new mower. Runyan says to put up plenty of hay. Seems like we
get more winter up here 'cause we're closer to the mountains."

Bronco fed his horse and stepped outside. "A lot to do and a
lot to learn." He nodded at the rim to the south. "Runyan says to
build rock fences in the breaks of that rim so our stock won't drift
south. Same down there at the mouth of the valley. Tomorrow

I'll take the wagon and go to the fort. We need more grub, and I want to see about having lumber sawed for the house."

"Let's eat," Mark said. "I figured you'd be home tonight."

Bronco laughed and slapped Mark a great blow on the back. "Home! Damned if that word don't have a good sound to it."

Mark could not bring himself to mention Jackson's visit until after they had finished supper. Then he said: "Herb Jackson was here yesterday."

"Yeah?" Bronco seemed surprised. "What'd he want?"

"He was looking for Orry Andrews. Said Andrews wouldn't leave the country without saying good bye, but Jackson hadn't seen anything of Andrews."

"Well, was that our fault? What was he getting at?"

"He didn't come right out and say. I told him Andrews sold out to you and left that same morning, and you'd gone with him from here."

Bronco shrugged as if it didn't matter. "It's none of my business what Andrews done or where he went after he left here. As far as I'm concerned, Jackson can stay on his side of the hills. He looked like an old maid to me. John Runyan's different. He's the kind of man I'm gonna be. Just give me time. When I come back from Winnemucca, I'll ride up along the west side of Shadow Mountain and visit Rocking Chair. I hear it's as big as the Triangle R, and Dave Nolan's a man like Runyan. Runyan's been in the country for eight years, Nolan six. I dunno about Matt Ardell on Bearpaw, but he's a hell of a long ways from here. I'll see him some other time."

Bronco got up and went to the bed. He fell across it as if he were too tired to sit. "Get started cutting wood?"

"No."

"Well, you cleaned the place up good. We'll make out this winter. Next spring we'll show Runyan and Nolan what it is to grow. We'll do in one year what they've done in six and eight.

Runyan said we could keep four, maybe five thousand head of cattle here. We'll never get as big as the Triangle R 'cause we ain't got as much range as Runyan's got, but we'll be big enough."

He sat up and tugged off his boots, then fell back on the bed again. "Mister, I'm tired." He sat up again. "Mark, we ain't gonna be living off the fat of the land for a while, but the day will come when we'll get our pay. How about it? You gonna stay with me?"

Mark had started to clear the table. He stopped to look at Bronco, a little surprised at the question. He had never forgotten that night on Crooked River when Bronco had called him a wet-nosed kid. Well, he had been, but he wasn't now.

Irritated by his hesitation, Bronco said: "I suppose I'll come back some night and find you gone."

"I was just thinking," Mark said. "You were pretty sore once about having to nurse a wet-nosed kid. . . ."

"So that's what's eating you. Hell, you were then, but you had enough savvy to learn. I've seen kids raised in the Willamette Valley. Nine times out of ten they can't make the grade over here. You can. I want somebody to stay here while I'm sashaying around. Somebody I can trust. I can't pay you anything now, but I'm not paying myself, neither. You can see how it is. I've got ten places to put every dollar I've got. A bed to sleep in and something to eat. That's all I've got to offer and all I can pay myself. How about it?"

Mark sat down at the table and rubbed his forehead. Strange how his memory had been stirred by what Bronco had said. He remembered his hopes and dreams, and those of his father, and how his mother had not wanted to come but hadn't really objected, either, because she was willing to do what her husband wanted.

He remembered how green and cool the Willamette Valley had been, how his mother had cried when they'd left the farm, but to him and his father the trip had been a new and wonderful adventure from the day they had started. Then that night on the Deschutes when they had almost reached the destination. . . .

He got up and walked to the door. Night now, the south rim looking like a heavy pencil line drawn across the low edge of the sky. The day had been hot and dry. Even with the sun down, the wind carried the heat down the valley, stirring the air but bringing little relief. The creek was so low he could hardly hear it. The coyotes were starting their night song, the sound coming clearly to him.

He turned to Bronco. "I'll be here," he said. That was all. Bronco nodded and lay back on the bed.

Later, when Mark lay beside Bronco on the bed, he considered this decision he had made. "Partner," Bronco had called him, and he nearly always said "we" instead of "I." But the arrangement had its bad points, too. Indirectly Mark would be responsible for anything Bronco did. The thought made him uneasy, for he could not forget that Bronco had called himself a getting man.

Mark had a nightmare that night. He was looking into the wagon again and seeing his parents with blood all over them, and he was crying out: "They're dead. They're dead." Bronco shook him awake. "Damn it, let a man sleep," he said in a cranky voice, and Mark laid back again, wet with sweat and tired and very lonely.

For some reason the loneliness lingered whether Bronco was home or not. They worked like madmen, Bronco always on the run and hating the time it took to bring a load of supplies from the fort. He'd spoken for the lumber next spring. Doors and windows, too. They'd have a fine house and good barn, he said, and one of these days he'd find a woman.

Mark started cutting the smaller pines on the hill above the house for wood, and Bronco helped him when he got back from the store. Then it was time to gather the cattle, and both were in the saddle from sunup to sundown. Bronco picked out twenty-eight Cross Seven steers to take to Winnemucca. The rest of the cattle were in good shape, the calves big and healthy.

"Even with the cold weather," Bronco said, "we'll get a good calf crop. That's why these California men come here. A lot more disease where it's warm, anthrax and such. Runyan was telling about a man named Jacob Smith. I'd heard about him. He's a big California cattleman, a millionaire, I guess. He shows up in Winnemucca every fall and buys and ships to California. Last year he told Andrews he'd never seen bigger steers than the ones Andrews shipped. I reckon we won't have any trouble selling the little jag we've got."

Mark found the constant riding hard work, but he enjoyed it until the last day, when they took a final swing into the mountains to be sure they hadn't missed a bunch that might have been hiding in the brush. They were five miles north of Ten Mile Valley in heavy timber when they ran into Herb Jackson, Jackson as surprised as they were.

They reined up, Bronco demanding: "What are you doing on Cross Seven range?"

The question was not a civil one, and it wasn't asked in a civil tone. Jackson was silent for a moment, looking at Bronco, and then at Mark. He seemed a little more stooped and a little grayer than the last time Mark had seen him, when Bronco was gone. Jackson wasn't armed, Mark saw, but if he was frightened or worried, he did not show it.

"I'm looking for Orry Andrews," he said. "Where did you bury him?"

Mark was not surprised at the question, but Bronco was. His dark face turned almost purple in a violent burst of rage, and he shouted: "What kind of god-damned question is that?"

Jackson was either stupid or brave. Mark wasn't sure which, but he decided it didn't make any difference because this was going to wind up in a killing if Mark didn't stop it. He eased his rifle out of the boot as Jackson said: "I knew Orry Andrews well. I was his only neighbor, and we visited back and forth once a week or more from the time Ruth and I moved here three years ago. I am not surprised he sold to you, but, having sold, he would never have left the country without seeing Ruth and me. He didn't show up, Curtis. He would have if he'd left Cross Seven range alive. I believe you killed him, took the money you'd given him for his property, and buried him up here in the mountains."

"I suppose I buried his horse and saddle, too," Bronco said.

"Perhaps," Jackson agreed. "I know I'm looking for a needle in a haystack because you probably buried him well, but, if I find him, I'll see you hang for it."

"You won't prove nothing if you do find him," Bronco said hotly. "Someone else might have done it."

"I know I didn't kill him," Jackson said, "and there's no one else except the boy." He nodded at Mark. "I'm sure he didn't. Even if Andrews had run into somebody else, he wouldn't have been killed for money because you were the only one who knew he had it."

Bronco had held his anger in check, but now it got away from him. He drew his gun, shouting: "You son-of-a-bitch, you're not going around telling them lies to nobody else!"

"Don't, Bronco," Mark said.

Bronco turned his head to look at the rifle in Mark's hands. It was lined on his belly. He asked incredulously: "You'd kill me to save this bastard's hide?"

"I'll kill you to keep you from murdering a man," Mark said.

Bronco wet his lips and nodded at Jackson. "Get out of here. Don't ever let me see you on Cross Seven range again."

Jackson wheeled his horse and disappeared into the timber. As Mark slipped the rifle back into the boot, Bronco said in a low voice: "I ought to beat hell out of you."

"Don't try it," Mark said. "You're big enough to do it, but, if you do, you'd better kill me. If you don't, I'll kill you. I agreed to stay here and work. I didn't agree to take any whippings."

Bronco laughed, the anger leaving him. "By God, I believe you would. I knew you had some sand in your craw. Just tell me one thing. Why did you keep me from beefing Jackson?"

"You figure on building a big outfit here," Mark said. "You told me I was your partner. I've got a stake to protect, haven't I? If you'd shot him, you couldn't have stayed."

"Why not?"

"One man might disappear on Cross Seven range and not make trouble, but a second man would start people asking questions. Besides, Jackson's got a daughter. She'd kick up a fuss if nobody else did."

"Makes sense." Bronco studied Mark a moment, then asked: "You don't think I plugged Andrews and took the money?"

Mark shook his head. "I wouldn't be staying if I did."

"I was sure gonna plug Jackson," Bronco said. "You knew it, or you wouldn't have jerked your rifle out."

"Killing a man when you're mad is one thing," Mark said, "but you weren't mad at Andrews. Shooting a man for his money is cold-blooded murder, and I don't figure you could do it."

"That's right," Bronco said. "I couldn't. Well, let's see if we missed any of our steers yesterday."

In spite of his assurance that he didn't believe Bronco had shot Andrews, questions began piling up in Mark's mind. He liked and trusted Jackson. He wasn't sure why unless it was because he sensed a simple honesty about the man that reminded him of his father.

On the other hand, he realized how ruthless the drive in Bronco Curtis was. He knew where he wanted to go, and he had to get there fast. Now Mark remembered how worried he had been when he had ridden with Bronco to Jackson's ranch and he had expected Bronco to force Jackson to sell.

The truth was Bronco needed working capital. If he had used all of his money to pay Andrews, the temptation would have been strong to take it back. Maybe he hadn't intended to kill the man; maybe Andrews had resisted and had tried to kill Bronco, and Bronco had shot him to save his own life. But that was no excuse if it had happened that way. The one big inescapable fact that Mark could not overlook was Jackson's insistence that Andrews had not stopped to say good bye.

They were friends. Jackson was certain Andrews would have stopped if he had been alive. Why hadn't he? And if Jackson was right, who besides Bronco would have shot Andrews? Was it possible that some drifter going through the country had stumbled onto Andrews and killed him? Mark didn't think so. Andrews didn't look like a man who would be carrying $3,000, and no one had known about the sale of his ranch except Mark and Bronco.

So the questions grew until they became staggering doubts and Mark knew he could not let the matter go. After supper he asked: "Where did Andrews go after you left him?"

Bronco stared at Mark a long moment before he answered, his dark face showing surprise and then hurt. Finally he said: "Well, by God, you lied. You told me you didn't think I shot Andrews and took the money, but you didn't mean a damned word of it, did you?"

Mark felt his face burn, but he said doggedly: "I asked a question. I've got a right to an answer."

"All right, I'll give you one." Bronco rose, so angry it was difficult for him to speak. "The last I saw of him he was riding north through the timber. I reckon he was heading for Cañon City. Don't ask me why he didn't tell Jackson good bye. I don't know. Maybe he figured Jackson would ask to borrow some of the *dinero*, and he didn't want to turn Jackson down. All I know is that Jackson's sore because Andrews didn't stop on his way out of the country, so he's trying to ease his own pride by making me out a back-shooting killer."

Then Bronco's temper roared away from him, and he slapped the table with the palm of his hand. "I won't have a partner who don't believe me. If you think I'm a liar, get to hell out of here. You've got your choice, boy. It's me or Jackson."

For a moment Mark's eyes met Bronco's angry ones, and suddenly he was ashamed as he remembered how much he owed Bronco. Mark had never known Bronco to lie. Andrews could have done exactly what Bronco had said. Until there was evidence that proved him guilty, Mark had to believe him.

"I don't think you're a liar," Mark said. "I just had to know."

"All right," Bronco said sullenly. "I don't want to hear another word about it, and I don't want to ever see Herb Jackson on Cross Seven range again. If you see him, tell him."

"I'll tell him," Mark said.

That was the end of it, Mark thought. He believed Bronco. If you lived with a man and you worked with him and you called him your partner, you had to believe him.

The next day Mark helped drive the twenty-eight steers as far south as the shoulder of Shadow Mountain, then Bronco sent him back, saying it was open country from there to the Triangle R and he could manage.

The last of the week Ruth Jackson rode to the Cross Seven. She heard Mark cutting wood on the hill and hunted until she found him. He straightened, releasing the handle of the cross-cut saw, and took off his hat. He said: "Sure good to see someone. Won't you get down?"

She shook her head, smiling at him, her cheeks bright from the cold. She was wearing a leather jacket over her blouse and on her head a red scarf, which hid most of her black hair.

"I can't stay," she said. "It'll be almost dark when I get home."

She was silent a moment, looking at the wood he'd cut, and it seemed to him she wasn't as shy as she had been when he'd eaten supper in her house. She was prettier, too, with the color in her cheeks, and suddenly the loneliness that had plagued him these last weeks was in him again.

He had a wild and crazy desire to ask her to stay with him until Bronco came back, or to let him go home with her. Instead, he compromised by asking: "Would it be all right if I came to see you?" Then he added quickly: "And your father?"

"It would be all right," she said. "Pa would be glad to see you." His question had made her shy again, and she glanced away. "Is Curtis here?"

"No, he took our steers south."

"I'm glad. I didn't want to see him. Pa said Curtis would have killed him if it hadn't been for you. I came over to thank you for saving Pa's life."

"No need for thanks," Mark said. "I couldn't let Bronco do it."

"Will you have dinner with us Sunday?" she asked. "Tomorrow?"

He had not realized the next day was Sunday. One day had been like another for so long that he had stopped wondering what day in the week it was. Once more childhood memories crowded into his mind. He had gone to Albany with his parents every Sunday to church.

"I'd like to come," he said. "Thank you."

"We'll look for you," she said, and rode away.

He sat down on the log and watched her as long as he could see her, a trim, graceful figure in the saddle. A lump crowded up into his throat so he couldn't swallow. Strange how some things reminded him of his folks and his home in the Willamette Valley, more now than during the summer when he'd been riding every day with Bronco.

Maybe it was because he was alone so much lately. Or maybe it was because he was over the shock and now fully realized that his boyhood was gone. He had to make his own life, and wasn't sure, even yet, that the life he wanted was here with Bronco Curtis.

He could not bear to sit and remember. He jumped up, grabbed the handle of the cross-cut, and feverishly attacked the log.

Chapter Eight

Mark rode into the Jackson yard shortly before noon. Herb Jackson met him and shook hands with him after he had dismounted, and walked beside him to the corral. He asked: "Curtis go south with the Triangle R drive?"

Mark nodded as he stripped gear from his sorrel and turned him into the corral. "We only had twenty-eight steers to go. I guess Runyan was glad to have an extra hand, and I don't suppose it's any more trouble to take our twenty-eight along than it would be to go without them."

"No, it isn't," Jackson said. "Right there is where the rest of us little fellows are in a bind. I've been lucky enough to sell a few steers at the fort, but it isn't a big market, and there are a lot of us in the hills trying to sell to the military."

"What do you mean, you're in a bind?"

"We don't have a big neighbor like John Runyan who'll take our stock like he takes the Cross Seven," Jackson answered. "He always took Andrews's, so he probably figured he would go on the same with whoever bought Cross Seven. I don't know what his object is unless he just wants to keep Curtis happy so he won't steal Triangle R cows."

"All of you in Sherman Valley could throw in together," Mark said. "The small outfits, I mean."

"We'd still have a small herd," Jackson said. "We don't know the buyers at Winnemucca, so we'd have trouble selling. But the big obstacle is the fact that there isn't any route we can follow unless we swing west over the high desert. And we'd lose our herd if we did that. Not enough water. You see, neither Dave Nolan nor Matt Ardell will let us drive across their ranges. I don't suppose Runyan would, either, but that's beside the point. It would be too far out of our way to go through Triangle R."

They started toward the house, Jackson silent for a moment, before he said: "I sent Ruth to invite you to dinner because she'd be safe. I wasn't sure Curtis would be gone. After he told me to stay off Cross Seven range, I knew what would happen if I showed up."

He glanced at Mark, smiling faintly. "I was foolish to accuse him the way I did. I wasn't armed, and, knowing he'd killed Orry Andrews, I should have realized he'd kill me. The truth is I didn't think that far. I just had the idea that, if I threw it in his teeth, he'd get jumpy enough to admit the killing. Well, if you hadn't been there, I'd be a dead man. So I wanted to thank you."

"That's all right," Mark said, embarrassed. "I hated to throw a gun on my partner, but I couldn't let him kill you."

"Partner?" Jackson said, his brows lifting.

"He calls me that," Mark said.

Jackson showed his doubt and let it drop there. He said: "I think dinner's about ready. Let's wash up and not keep Ruth waiting. She gets a little impatient with me sometimes."

They washed, then Mark found a comb stuck between two logs and ran it through his hair. It didn't do much good, even though he had sloshed water on his hair. It flared back up, as stiff as a horse's tail. He turned from the mirror, disgusted.

He looked like a tramp. He didn't even own a decent-looking shirt. Jackson's shirt had been ironed, and he remembered how his mother used to iron his clothes with meticulous care. But that, he told himself, was something else that belonged to his past.

Ruth called them to dinner. Mark spoke to her as he went into the kitchen, and she smiled and spoke to him, and he thought she had lost the shyness he had sensed the first time he'd seen her. She was wearing a dark blue skirt, a blouse of lighter blue, and a white apron over her skirt, and with her black hair pinned on top of her head in a sort of coronet she seemed very tall.

She was a woman, Mark thought as he sat down at the table, a woman who wouldn't remain single long in a country where wives were hard to get. The thought bothered him as he ate. It would be a long time before he could take a wife, and he would be a fool even to think of asking her to wait.

Ruth's good dinner took his mind off his troubled thoughts. Fried chicken, gravy, potatoes, carrots, and biscuits, and for dessert a three-layer cake with some kind of custard filling that was, as his father used to say "lickin' good."

He ate until he was ashamed of himself. He sat back at last, looking at Ruth and shaking his head as she offered him a third helping of cake. "I just can't hold any more," he said. "I do most of the cooking whether Bronco's home or not, but it sure doesn't taste like this."

"She's the best dog-goned cook in the valley," Jackson bragged. "She's got a lot of accomplishments, come to think of it. She's a good hand with cattle . . ."

"Pa," Ruth said angrily. "You hush up."

Jackson spread his hands and laughed again. "All right, but I'm not one to hide your light under a basket."

A strained silence followed, Ruth's face going scarlet. Finally Mark said: "It was an awful good dinner. Trouble with my cooking is that it gets monotonous. It's beans and sage hen, or beans and antelope, or beans and venison."

Laughing, Ruth asked: "Can't you make biscuits?"

"Sure. When we get short of ammunition, I throw the biscuits at the sage hens. They're better than rocks."

"And for variety you have sage hen and beans, antelope and beans, and venison and beans," Ruth said.

"That's right," Mark agreed, and they all laughed.

Jackson rose. "Let's go out on the front porch and sit."

Mark followed Jackson through the front room. The furniture was comfortable and adequate: a lamp with a dark red shade on a claw-footed oak table, a bookcase filled with books, a haircloth-covered sofa, and a cane-seated rocker. The floor was of planks, many of them warped, but Ruth had hidden much of the roughness of the floor with rag rugs. The log walls were covered with white cheesecloth, and on this she had pinned pictures and poems, which she had cut from magazines.

The familiar lump was in Mark's throat again as he sat down beside Jackson on the front porch. Ruth had a way of doing much with little. The result was that this log house had a homey feeling Mark had not felt anywhere since he had left the Willamette Valley. Bronco Curtis could build his fine house next summer, Mark thought, but it would never have the homey atmosphere this place did.

Jackson filled his pipe, nodding at the valley below him, which ran so far to the south that the sky seemed to bend down to touch the land. Shadow Mountain, the one tall peak that could be seen from the Jackson porch, had a scarf of new snow.

It would not be long until there was snow in the foothills of the Blue Mountains, too, Mark thought, and then it would be in the valley. Many winters in the Willamette Valley there was no snow at all, and Mark wondered how it would be here and if he could stand the cold.

"Folks asked why I picked this spot," Jackson said, "when I could have settled down there in the valley where the grass is better and you can get three times as much wild hay to an acre. I'm not very practical, Mark. People have always called me a dreamer, and I'm afraid they're right. The truth is I like it up here where I can look at the valley." He laughed, and added: "You know, a man can always see the sun longer when he lives on a mountain than if he lives in the valley."

He tamped tobacco into the bowl of his pipe, then lit it and pulled hard on it. With the pipe stem between his teeth, he went on: "I'm not practical, you see, or I wouldn't have spent days hunting Orry Andrews's grave. I always have work to do, and Ruth's mad at me because I haven't been doing it."

He puffed for a moment, his eyes on the valley, then he said: "There are times, as I ride through the hills, when I feel that all the wisdom of God and man is pressing upon me, yet I am not capable of tapping it. But I do believe that every man must have a philosophy to live by. Mine is the notion that man will find his fate from his hopes, but most of us look to our fears, which stop us. I suppose that none of us will ever understand the plan of which we are a part, and that is a great tragedy."

He took the pipe out of his mouth and frowned at the ash in the bowl. "I must apologize to you, my young friend. Ruth warned me not to bore you with my talk." He struck a match and lit his pipe again. "How old are you, Mark?"

"Nineteen. I had a birthday last month."

"Ruth's almost eighteen. She was just a child when her mother died. She has taken care of me ever since. The exigencies of life force maturity upon youth too early in many cases, especially in a pioneer community like this." He pulled on his pipe, eyes on the far horizon, then he asked: "How did you get involved with a man like Bronco Curtis?"

Mark liked neither the way Jackson worded the question nor the tone in which he said it. "He's not an evil man, Mister Jackson. You're hinting that he is. You don't actually know he killed Orry Andrews."

"Evil is a matter of interpretation, Mark," Jackson said, ignoring what Mark had said about Andrews's killing.

"You don't know he killed Andrews," Mark insisted.

"Ah, I know it well enough," Jackson said, "but I can't prove it, so I'll drop it for the time being."

"My father used to say that a man was innocent until he was proved guilty in court."

Jackson smiled. "So your father was a dreamer, too. The world is full of them, and Bronco Curtis is included, although his dreams are different from mine and your father's. He's a young man in a hurry. He wants to go too far too fast. Isn't that right?"

Mark nodded and thought about it a moment. Then he said: "But you still haven't proved he murdered Orry Andrews."

Jackson shrugged. "You saw with your own eyes his obvious intention of murdering me. You wouldn't have put your rifle on him if you hadn't been aware of his intention. And once he has the wealth and the power that wealth gives a man, he will be exactly like John Runyan and Dave Nolan and Matt Ardell. Like them, he will be guilty of any crime he feels he must commit to hold grass he claims but does not legally own."

Jackson pointed a forefinger at Mark to emphasize his point. "Fraud can be legal, you know, if you interpret the word *legal* loosely. For instance, the big cowmen all own vast amounts of land they have bought from the state as swamp land but that is not swamp at all." He stopped and seemed embarrassed. "There I go again, and I didn't intend to. Tell me how you and Curtis got together."

Mark didn't want to because it would only sharpen his memory and he had tried to blunt it, but he could think of no reason not to talk that would seem plausible to Jackson, so he told him the story, and Jackson nodded from time to time as he listened closely.

When Mark had finished, Jackson said: "I can understand why you are loyal to Curtis. It would not speak well of your character if you felt otherwise. I can only hope you will hold to your own convictions of what is right and what is wrong." He knocked the pipe out against the heel of his boot. "The thing I wonder about is why he was so anxious to get Malone out of

Prineville that day. We can only be sure of one thing. Curtis is a man who has reasons for everything he does."

Mark made no attempt to explain Bronco's action. The question had not really occurred to him before, and now he could think of no answer that seemed logical. Certainly Bronco's explanation that he didn't want to see Red Malone hanged was a poor one, because neither Bud Ackerman nor anyone else in Prineville seemed the kind who would lead a lynch mob.

Ruth appeared in the doorway, and Mark, glancing at the sun, jumped up. "Time I was moving."

"Wait till I put my riding skirt on," Ruth said, "and I'll ride a ways with you."

"I'll saddle your mare," Jackson said, and rose.

Mark was waiting in front of the house with his sorrel and the pinto mare Jackson had saddled when Ruth came out of the house. Mark called—"So long!"—to Jackson, who stood by the corral gate. He helped Ruth mount, then stepped into the saddle.

"I'll beat you to the road," Ruth said, and was off in a run.

She made good her brag, beating him by a full length, and, when they pulled down to a walk and turned east, she laughed at him, a strand of black hair that had come loose dangling against her forehead.

"See?" she said. "I'm a better rider than you are."

"No, you're not," he said. "And your mare isn't as fast as my sorrel. You just got the jump on me."

"Alibis, alibis," she said, laughing. Then the smile left her face, and she added: "Pa talked your leg off, didn't he? I don't know what gets into him when he finds a listener. As he says, he gets intoxicated on his own verbiage."

"It was all right," he said. "I enjoyed listening to him."

They rode in silence until they reached the summit of the range of hills, then she drew up. "I'll have to go back."

He pulled his sorrel to a stop, looking at her and thinking of the lonely days that lay ahead for him. He said: "I've enjoyed having somebody to talk to, and I sure did like the dinner."

"Pa and I were glad to have you," she said. "It's a lonesome country, and we don't have many friends. Orry Andrews was the only one Pa had, and I don't have anyone except Missus Bolton at the fort."

He realized she was lonely, too, and he was surprised by the discovery. He wanted to reach out and touch her; he felt a desire to kiss her, but she'd probably slap his face.

"I'll come and see you if Bronco doesn't get sore about it," he said. "I don't want to make more trouble between him and your pa."

"I understand," she said. Then she wheeled her mare and started back down the west slope, calling: "So long!"

"So long!" he said, turning in the saddle. He watched her for a long time, then rode home, hating the dismal prospect of being alone, and knowing that even when Bronco returned, the loneliness would not be entirely dispelled.

* * * * *

By the time Bronco rode in two weeks later, the weather had turned cold and snow reached as far as the ridge where Mark was cutting wood. Bronco was wearing a new sheepskin and had brought one for Mark. He tossed it to Mark, saying: "You won't freeze in that, boy, and you're sure gonna need it before summer."

He was just as exuberant as he had been the time he returned from the Triangle R. He'd visited Dave Nolan's Rocking Chair, but he hadn't liked Nolan as well as Runyan. Too precise, too calculating, but he'd been friendly enough, and he was a good cowman. His spread was bigger, even, than Runyan's Triangle R.

"But the real news is that we're fixed," Bronco said. "Remember I told you about the big California cowman named Jacob Smith who buys at Winnemucca and ships to the coast? Well, he was there, and I had a talk with him. I got top price for our twenty-eight head. I made him a proposition after telling him we had a paradise for cows here. Drive a cow-and-calf herd north next summer and we'll split the profits. By God, Mark, I put it over. He took me up on it, and we'll be in business five years sooner than we expected. He even loaned me some money to get the place fixed up before summer."

He scratched the back of his neck, sobering. "There's just one hitch. He wants to know how we make out this winter and how good a calf crop we get before he backs us. So we've got to work like hell and show him we can bring our stock through the winter no matter how tough it is."

Mark didn't mention the Jacksons until after supper, when Bronco was sitting in front of the stove with his boots off, a cigarette dangling from one corner of his mouth, his forehead creased by his thinking and scheming.

Mark said: "I ate Sunday dinner with the Jacksons, and they asked me to come back to see them."

Bronco straightened and grabbed the cigarette out of his mouth. "I thought you were going to stay away from 'em."

"I don't know why I should. I like Ruth."

Bronco laughed shortly. "I forgot about the girl. Natural enough for you to see her, but you stay away from her lying old man. Savvy?"

Mark nodded, and turned away. It was what he had expected, and something he had been prepared to accept. No matter how much he wanted to see Ruth, he couldn't endanger her father, and eventually that was what he would do if he visited Ruth.

Chapter Nine

The winter was a mild one. The valley had not been over-grazed, and with the snow going off the ground soon after each storm, the tall bunch grass on the upper slopes of the valley was available to the cattle almost every day.

As it turned out, the small amount of hay that Andrews had put up was ample, but it would have been a different story if the weather had been severe. Bronco admitted to Mark that their ability to bring cattle through a hard winter had not been tested, but there was nothing to be gained by telling Jacob Smith that.

Once the winter's supply of wood had been cut and hauled to the cabin, it fell to Mark to do the chores and the cooking. Bronco worked hard and expected hard work from Mark when he wasn't busy in the cabin or barn. They spent most of the time through the first half of the winter building rock fences in the breaks of the south rim.

"Andrews would have got this done if he hadn't been so lazy," Bronco said. "It'll pay us, all right. Works both ways. It'll keep our cattle on our grass, and everybody else's off."

Bronco put up signs on the west, south, and east sides of the valley saying this was Cross Seven range. At the time, with so few people in the country, there was little to worry about. Triangle R was too far to the south, and there were no ranches between Ten Mile Valley and the Paiute reservation to the east. The mountains on the north furnished summer graze, but little more, so no one was likely to settle there.

"Just looking ahead," Bronco said. "If anybody tries to settle on our grass or shoves their cattle onto Cross Seven range, they're going to be smelling powder smoke." He grinned and winked. "That is, if they live long enough to smell anything."

Mark knew Bronco was thinking of Herb Jackson. If his Circle J stock drifted across the Paradise Hills, there would be trouble, and Bronco would welcome it. He had not forgiven Jackson for his accusation.

Bronco made occasional trips to the fort, but he didn't take Mark. If Bronco ever ran into Jackson, he didn't mention it. Neither Jackson nor Ruth came to the Cross Seven during the winter, and Mark got no closer to the Circle J than the summit of the Paradise Hills. There he would sit his saddle, looking down upon the Jackson house, hoping to glimpse Ruth, but he never did.

Christmas came and went, Mark not sure which day it was. Even if they had known, it would have been only another work day to Bronco, but it would have meant a great deal to Mark. Again the memories from his boyhood flooded his mind.

At night he lay awake thinking of the tiny fir trees he had always picked for his father to cut in the pasture above the barn, and how they trimmed them with their homemade ornaments and the little candles that were lighted only on Christmas Eve. That was when they opened the packages, but now, thinking back, Mark did not remember many of the presents. What he did remember was the rich feeling of love and good will to all men and how his parents kissed each other as they opened their presents.

He remembered, too, the Christmas program at the schoolhouse, and how they nearly always traveled through misty rain from their home with mud sucking at the horses' hoofs, and how he usually recited a poem on which his mother had drilled him for days, and how his father was the Santa Claus with his red suit and white beard and the pillows under his shirt and pants to give him the big belly Santa Claus must have. There would be at least one present for each child, maybe a picture book for Mark, and an orange, the only one he'd get all year, a treasure to be cherished. Even now his mouth would water as he remembered the tangy, juicy taste.

Several times in December he had the nightmare again, and he'd sit up in bed, sweating and tense as he screamed: "They're dead! They're dead!" Or he would relive the scene in Prineville when he had heard Red Malone's voice and he was trying to get the rifle out of the boot and he was screaming at Ackerman to come and get Malone. Then Bronco would shake him awake and curse him and tell him they were in bed to sleep.

After that he would lie awake, trembling and tired, and think of the Jacksons, who would have some kind of Christmas, for they were people who would understand and appreciate this season of the year and its spirit, which Bronco would probably never know. Mark told himself he was going to marry Ruth. He'd go over and see her, and to hell with what Bronco thought. But he never went.

Next day, working beside Bronco under the pale winter sun, he realized how childish his dreams were. He had no money. Bronco had not paid him a cent of wages, and Mark was sure it would do no good to ask. How could he, a boy with only Bronco's promise of a great future, ask a girl to marry him? No, there was nothing to do but wait and run the risk of losing her.

For some reason Mark felt better in January, perhaps because Christmas was behind him and he had survived the loss of it. Always there was some pressing work. The creek almost stopped flowing, but there were several deep holes above the buildings, and the ice must be kept broken.

More corrals to be built. Gravel to be hauled to the corrals so if the spring was a wet one, the ground wouldn't be churned into a loblolly. Hay cribs to be built. Ditches to be dug so more ground could be flooded next summer and more hay raised.

Later in the winter there were a few heavy snows, and the cattle had to be fed. Then spring was upon them, with the snow going off the foothills and the grass beginning to show, and it was calving time.

After that, there was no time to dream, to have nightmares, or to conjure memories from a dead past. Bronco was like a machine that was too tightly wound. "We're not going to lose a calf," he said over and over to Mark. "By God, we'll show Jacob Smith what we can do."

Bronco had bought several extra saddle horses during the fall. Now he and Mark rode every daylight hour, keeping the cows close to the middle of the valley on clean pasture where they could be watched for calving signs. It was not such a difficult task with so few, but Mark wondered what it would be like if they had a thousand head ready to calve.

Still, it was work, and Mark was glad to have so much to do. He learned to know each cow. Most of them were driven into the corrals when they began to make bag. Usually the calves were born with little difficulty, but occasionally a cow had to be helped.

Since it was instinctive for a cow to hide out at such a time, Bronco gave Mark the job of watching the brush along the creek and the gullies that cut across the valley from the mountains for the few cows that had escaped. He rode with gunny sacks tied to his cantle, and on a few occasions he had to carry a new calf out of a brush pocket and rub it dry, for this was the in-between time, half spring, half winter, with an unexpected shower or snow squall coming at the wrong time.

When it was over, Bronco was pleased. "Not a hundred percent," he said, "but damn' near it. If we get Jacob Smith here this summer, we'll show him the best calves he ever saw."

"You can't work this way with a big herd," Mark said. "I got so I could tell you about every cow we've got right down to the kind of mother she is."

"And you've felt the horns of a few of 'em in your butt, haven't you?" Bronco laughed. "Learned to keep one eye on the calf and the other on the cow, didn't you?"

Mark was irritated, but he held his tongue. A few times when a cow had misunderstood his motives had been almost disastrous to him, but humorous to Bronco. Ignoring the question, Mark said: "Well, how about it? I'd like to see you and me nurse a thousand head the way we did the shirt tailful we've got now."

"We'll have some buckaroos to help," Bronco said. "Anyhow, it ain't anything I'm going to tell Jacob Smith. I'm just going to say we done good this spring and show him the percentage."

It was May then, with no snow visible from the valley and the sun warm enough to prove that summer was just around the corner. Late in the month two small bands of Paiutes rode through the valley, headed toward the reservation. Once Bronco was there and said just to ignore them. The other time he had gone to the fort, and Mark was alone. He ran into the house and shut and barred the door, then crouched at the window with his rifle in his hand.

Mark counted a dozen braves in the outfit, young ones as near as he could tell. They stopped on the other side of the creek, which was running high, and seemed to be carrying on an argument, but their voices were lost in the roar of the creek. Several pointed to the corral that held the horses.

Mark gripped his rifle so hard his hands ached. He hadn't seen anyone but Bronco all winter, and if Bronco had heard at the fort that an uprising was imminent, he hadn't mentioned it. Now Mark remembered hearing some talk last summer about the Indians being restless.

He had never been as frightened as he was at this moment. If they came after the horses, he had to stop them, but one rifle against a dozen made hopeless odds. They'd get him and the horses and probably burn the buildings, and then where would Bronco and his fine dreams be?

But nothing came of it. The Indians rode on, and, when they were out of sight beyond the gap at the east end of the valley, Mark opened the door and sat down, so weak his knees refused to hold him. He probably couldn't have hit one of them if he'd tried.

He didn't get any sympathy from Bronco when he told him that evening. Bronco slapped him on the back as he laughed, and said: "You're as good as a regiment. They knew you were forted up in here, and they didn't want the horses bad enough to get shot to hell."

"Damn it, what have you heard at the fort?" Mark demanded. "You don't tell me anything."

"I don't know nothing," Bronco said, "but I'll stick around close if you'll feel any better. We're going to have to start branding in a little while. I've been thinking some of putting in a garden, but I guess that's too much to do. Maybe you'd better start getting in next winter's wood. We'll use three times as much with our new house, a cook shack, and a bunkhouse."

Mark didn't feel any better with Bronco home. Two rifles were twice as good as one, but they still made short odds against a dozen Indians. For several days nothing happened, and he began to think he was excited over nothing. Bronco had told him before that with the Cross Seven so close to the reservation, they were bound to have a few Paiute visitors, and maybe that was all it amounted to.

But late in the month he learned it was more than that. A military courier headed for Camp Sherman rode through the valley and stopped long enough to tell Mark and Bronco that the

Bannocks in Idaho had gone on the warpath and were headed toward Oregon.

After the courier had gone on, Bronco made light of the whole business. "These are Paiutes. Hell, they're just Digger Indians. They won't fight. Anyhow, the military will stop the Bannocks before they get to the Oregon line."

He might be right, Mark thought, but he wasn't sure. Bronco would naturally look at it this way. He wasn't one to run off and leave his horses to be stolen without a fight and maybe have his cattle butchered and the buildings burned. Not that they amounted to much, but they'd do until the lumber was hauled from the sawmill and the carpenters arrived from the Triangle R.

That was the way it stood until early in June when Monk Evans, a buckaroo from the Triangle R, rode in on a lathered horse with news that the Bannocks had reached Shadow Mountain and had been joined by most of the Paiutes from the reservation.

The Bannock chief, Buffalo Horn, had been killed in a fight near the Oregon-Idaho line, and several isolated ranches had been burned and a stage driver killed. Runyan and his crew were headed for the fort, and Evans had been sent to warn Bronco and Mark.

"Thanks, Monk," Bronco said, "but we're a long ways from Shadow Mountain. I reckon they won't come this way."

"You can lose your scalp if you've a mind to," Evans said, "but I'm going to the fort. I want a fresh horse."

"Sure, you can have one," Bronco said affably, and walked to the corral with him.

In five minutes Evans was on his way and Bronco returned to the cabin. He looked at Mark and grinned. "It just goes to show that if a man has money and knows he can start over again, he'll think enough of his skin to keep it in one piece, but, if we lose what we've got, we might just as well go to work for thirty a month and beans."

Mark, staring at Bronco's expressionless face, knew there was no use to argue, that the Cross Seven meant more to Bronco than his own life, but Mark could not keep from saying: "What good is a ranch to a dead man?"

"If you're scared," Bronco said, "saddle your sorrel and light out for the fort."

Mark shook his head. "I'm staying if you are."

"Good," Bronco approved. "I'll tell you what. We'll head for the fort the first time we hear an Indian gun pop. I don't think we will. Indian scare talk is like a grass fire. Spreads like hell when it starts."

That, Mark thought, was a bigger concession than he had expected to get from Bronco Curtis, and it was proof that he honestly believed there would be no serious trouble.

Chapter Ten

Through the days following Monk Evans's warning, both Mark and Bronco rode with revolvers in their holsters and rifles in the boots. They watched the rim to the south and the brush along the creek and the wooded hills to the north. At night they blanketed the windows so no light showed, they barred the door, and, when they slept, they kept their rifles and revolvers close to the bed.

"I ain't scared, you understand," Bronco told Mark. "I can handle a dozen Paiutes myself. You might even be able to take care of one or two."

"For a man who isn't scared," Mark said, "you're mighty careful."

"Careful," Bronco repeated, and grinned. "That's the right word. A careful man lives longer'n one who ain't, and I've got a hell of a lot to live for."

Mark worried about the Jacksons, but he told himself he had no reason to be concerned. Monk Evans would certainly have stopped at the Jackson place on his way to the fort. If they chose to stay home, that was their privilege. Besides, it was unlikely that a raiding band of Paiutes would attack a ranch in Sherman Valley, at least one as close to the fort as the Circle J.

Bronco kept Mark so busy there was no time to visit the Jacksons. Still, he would have gone at night if there had been any doubt in his mind about their safety. He told himself that, if they hadn't believed Evans, they wouldn't believe him. No, they must be at the fort by now. Herb Jackson had more to lose than Bronco, but he wasn't bull-headed.

Each night when they came home and turned their horses into the corral, Bronco said: "Guess the Indian scare's over. We can leave our guns at home tomorrow." But the following morning he had his rifle and revolver with him as usual, apparently forgetting what he had said the night before.

On the fourth evening before they went to bed, Bronco said: "I'm going to the fort tomorrow. This could go on till fall without us hearing what's happened. Chances are the Indians are all dead by now, and, if we don't get at the branding in a day or two, them calves will be so big you won't be able to wrestle 'em."

Bronco slept as wholeheartedly as he ate. It was the same this night, but not with Mark who would drop off to sleep and then wake up with a start a few minutes later. After that, he would lie there listening for sounds that weren't right.

For some reason he couldn't get his mind off Ruth. Every time he woke up, his first thought was of her. He knew that if she were murdered by the Indians, he would never forgive himself. He'd ride to the Circle J tomorrow when Bronco was gone and find out if the Jacksons were still there. He'd let it go too long now.

Usually Bronco and Mark got up before sunup, but they had been sleeping later than usual the last few mornings. With the window blanketed, the interior of the cabin remained dark, so they missed the first opalescent light of dawn, which normally got Bronco out of bed as effectively as an alarm clock.

Mark woke from one of his short naps with a strange, heart-thumping feeling that something was wrong. He lay on his back, listening to Bronco's rumbling snores and wishing they would stop for a moment. He had no notion of time, of whether it was dawn yet or not. If he woke Bronco and it was the middle of the night and nothing was wrong, he'd get a cussing and the usual admonition that they were in bed to sleep and there was work to be done tomorrow.

But Mark's heart kept pounding. He had a strange feeling in the back of his neck that made the short hairs stand straight out. He'd have a look, he decided, whether he woke Bronco or not.

Very carefully he eased out of bed and fumbled around in the darkness for his revolver on the floor. He found it, and discovered that the hard walnut butt of the gun gave him the assurance he needed. He slipped noiselessly across the room to the window, successfully circling the table and chairs without making any sound, and lifted the corner of the blanket.

Mark's breathing stopped as suddenly as if he'd been kicked in the stomach, and his heart went into a crazy pattern of thumping and missing and thumping and missing. In the uncertain light of dawn he saw two Paiutes bending over a pile of sagebrush and dry grass they had thrown against the wall of the cabin. A small flame was leaping up just as Mark lifted the blanket.

Under ordinary circumstance Mark would have called Bronco, but now he didn't even think of it. He fired through the window, the bullet going through one Indian's head and knocking him as flat as if he'd been hit by a club. The other one wheeled and started to run toward the creek. Mark's second shot was a clean miss. The Paiute kept going until a third bullet caught him between the shoulder blades and brought him down in a lurching fall.

In that short interval of time the flame had spread and doubled in height. Mark dropped his gun and, running to the door, lifted the bar and shoved the door open. Bronco was out of bed in a lunge, yelling: "What the hell's going on?"

By that time Mark was outside kicking the pile of sage and grass away from the cabin wall with his bare feet. He couldn't stomp the blaze out, but he succeeded in scattering the pile and getting it far enough from the log wall so that the fire sputtered and died.

"Get back inside, you fool!" Bronco yelled. "Get back!"

Mark leaped for the door just as firing broke out from the creek. He had a horrible, fleeting fear he wouldn't make it. There must be a hundred of them in the willows. He had never been shot at before; he had never heard a bullet that had been fired with the intention of killing him. But he did now. One snapped past his ear to go through the open door and slam into the log wall on the opposite side of the cabin. Another splintered the door casing. Others thudded into the log wall on both sides of the door.

Mark tripped and fell as a bullet ripped into the table in the middle of the room. He got to his hands and knees and lunged forward and rolled to one side as Bronco slammed the door shut and barred it, then yelled: "What the god damned hell is going on?"

Mark started to dress, his hands trembling so much he had trouble getting his shirt and pants buttoned. He said in a shaky voice: "They were firing the cabin. I got two of them."

"The hell you did." Bronco wheeled to the window and jerked the blanket down. "Seems like you did at that. The light ain't good, but looks like one of 'em is lying right here by the cabin. There's another one out there a piece, all right." He backed against the wall and faced Mark as he said with grudging respect: "If you hadn't woke up, we'd have fried in here just like two squirrels in a hole."

Mark had pulled on his boots and began buckling his gun belt around him. Rifles were still cracking from the brush along the creek, and now and then a bullet came singing through a window to scream as it ricocheted off the stove or made a dull sound as it buried itself into the wall.

"How many are out there?" Mark asked as he tugged his hat low over his forehead and filled his pockets with rifle shells from a box on a shelf beside the door.

"Six or eight." Bronco took a quick look through the window and jerked back against the wall again. "Well, kid, I guess you were right. A ranch don't do a dead man much good. Say, what are you fixing to do now?"

"I'm going out there," Mark said. "If we stay here, they'll get our horses. That's what they're after, isn't it?"

"You'll never make it from here to the corral," Bronco said. "Stay inside."

"We won't ever make it if we wait for it to get light," Mark said. "Do some shooting so they won't notice me."

Bronco swore angrily. "Wait'll I get dressed and I'll go with you."

"I can't wait," Mark snapped. "Chances are they've got the horses already."

He lifted the bar and jerked the door open and went through it on the run. Bronco opened up from the window, firing as rapidly as he could lever shells into the chamber. Mark headed for the corral that held the horses. The light was still too thin for accurate shooting, but before Mark had covered half the distance, the Indians hidden along the creek saw him and began firing.

Mark cut back and forth in a zigzag pattern, bending low and making a poor target even for good riflemen. Bronco's firing probably helped, for he was laying his bullets low just above the creekbank, and the screen of willows gave no protection.

Mark was so intent on reaching the corral that he didn't see the Indian on a paint pony that was trying to open the corral gate until he was almost upon him. Apparently the Paiute saw him the same instant, for he wheeled his pony and drove directly at Mark. Acting purely from instinct, Mark fell to one side and, tilting his rifle, pulled the trigger.

The Indian leaned down and made a sweep with an axe or a war club. Mark couldn't tell what it was. He glimpsed the brave's almost naked body and his painted face and knew the weapon would have split his skull if it had landed. It missed by inches.

Apparently Mark had creased the pony with his shot, for he was hard to manage and lunged on past Mark. This time Mark fired from his knees. The Paiute threw up his hands and came off the back of the paint in a rolling fall.

The pony kept on, past the barn and across the meadow above the buildings. The Indian was wounded and jarred by the fall, but he was still alive. He started to sit up, and this time Mark put a bullet into his brain.

Mark got up and ran toward the corner of the corral, bullets kicking up dirt around him. Inside the corral the horses, boogered by the firing, were snorting and running in circles. Mark went on past the corral to the barn and, jerking the door open, fell forward into the litter.

He lay there, panting and scared and exhausted, but at the same time he was filled with a wild exhilaration. He may have been a fool, and Bronco would probably call him one, but he had saved the horses. If he had been a few seconds later, the Indian would have had the gate open and the horses would have been gone. Then he and Bronco would have been on foot, and it was hard to tell what would have happened.

It took a long time to get his wind back. When he did, he sat up and reloaded his rifle. Then he didn't know what to do. Bronco was still in the cabin, and he was out here. What he had done so far had been right, but it had been on the spur of the moment. Now that he had time to think about his next move, he was confused. He crawled out of the barn to the corner of the corral and hunkered there, his eyes on the willows where the Indians were hiding.

The sun was beginning to show, a red arc above the hills that formed the eastern boundary of the valley. The light had deepened until he could see the willows clearly, but there was no movement. Maybe they were gone. He considered the possibility for a time, thinking that, if the Indians had made the raid strictly to get horses, they wouldn't stay.

An hour passed in silence except for an occasional shot that Bronco took from the window. Mark put his hat on his rifle barrel and shoved it around the corner of the corral. Nothing happened. He thought about standing up and stepping into view, but decided against it. The screen of willows was so thick that it was possible for them to be hidden, or to have fled without being seen. He just wasn't sure, but he had no desire to commit suicide.

Another plan occurred to him. A deep gully angled south to the creek not far to the west. If he could reach it, he could crawl to the creek and then follow the stream to where the Indians were hiding. Then he'd know if they were gone. He realized immediately it was an absurd plan. He couldn't reach it without being seen. If they were still hiding and he ran into the whole band, he'd die quickly and suddenly.

The horses had quieted inside the corral. Mark pulled his hat low over his eyes and waited, trying to think of something else. Bronco had not fired a shot for ten or fifteen minutes. Suddenly he broke out of the cabin and ran toward Mark, his rifle in his hand.

Halfway to the corral he stopped and faced the creek, standing straight up. Nothing happened, so he came on. It seemed to Mark that he was crazy to stop that way. Then it struck Mark that it had been an act of bravado to save face, that he'd probably seen the Indians leave and had kept up the pretense that they were still there by firing an occasional shot.

"I figured they were gone," he said, "but I wasn't sure."

Mark got to his feet and wiped the sweat from his face. "I've got time to be scared now, I guess."

"You got a right to be, boy," Bronco agreed. "I've been scared ever since you got off your first shot, and I jumped ten feet straight up off the bed." He put a hand on Mark's shoulder. "You done good, boy. Real good. That first one you plugged has got his brains scattered over half the yard."

Bronco turned to the corral and leaned his rifle against it. "I ain't as brave as I make out. Not when it comes to fighting ten or twelve of the devils and maybe getting my hair lifted. I've never met a white man I was scared of, but there's something about a bunch of damned Indians that drops my heart clean through my guts." He tried to grin. "It'll be different the next time I meet up with 'em."

"Why didn't they just take the horses and pull out?" Mark asked. "If they'd really wanted our hair, they'd have stayed."

Bronco shook his head. "Might've been different if it had been the Nez Percés. Or the Sioux. But them Paiutes ain't real good fighters. They wanted something easy like burning us out or plugging us when it got so hot inside the cabin we couldn't stay. Chances are they sent out a few raiding parties to pick up horses and any cheap scalps they could get, but we're a long ways from Shadow Mountain. Maybe the main band's on the move and these boogers who tackled us didn't want to be pinned down all day."

"And maybe," Mark said, "the main band is headed this way."

Bronco scratched his head and grinned sourly. "Like you said, a ranch ain't much good to a dead man. I made you a promise and I'll keep it. We'll head for the fort."

They saddled up, Mark taking his sorrel and Bronco a bay gelding, then they turned the rest of the horses out of the corral. They rode west toward the Paradise Hills, Mark looking back once and wondering if he would ever see the cabin again that had been his home since fall. He turned his head and looked at the hills before him, shiny bright with the morning sunlight upon them, and grew a little sick with the thought that, if the Indians came again, every building would be burned to the ground.

Chapter Eleven

When Mark crossed the Paradise Hills and came into sight of the Circle J buildings, he saw that they were intact and that smoke was rising from the chimney of the house. He swung off the trail, calling to Bronco: "I'm going to tell the Jacksons to go to the fort!"

Bronco motioned for Mark to come on. "Monk Evans told 'em. Let 'em stay if they want to!"

Mark kept on, shouting: "I'll catch up with you if they won't go!"

Bronco cursed and told him to let them go, but Mark didn't look back. He rode across the sage-covered bench, thinking it was natural that Bronco wouldn't want to have anything to do with Herb Jackson. Mark had worried a good deal during the winter about what would happen when they met, as they were bound to do sooner or later. But regardless of how Bronco felt about Herb, he shouldn't object to Mark's warning them, especially with Ruth at home. The more he thought about it, the more irritated he became over Bronco's attitude.

Mark didn't see anyone when he reached the house. He swung down and, leaving the reins dragging, ran to the front door and pounded on it. When there was no answer, he pounded on it again. Then the door opened and Ruth stood there, her hands on her hips.

"You're a long time coming," she said tartly, "and, when you do decide to come, you try to knock the door off its hinges."

He didn't notice her tartness. He was so relieved to see her that he grabbed her and hugged her, saying: "I guess you're all right. I've sure been worried. Why didn't you go to the fort?"

She took hold of his arms and, shoving them apart, stepped back. "I'll bet you've been worried about me. You haven't been over here all winter." Then she seemed to understand his question, and she demanded: "Why should we go to the fort?"

"Indians. Didn't Monk Evans warn you?"

"No. I don't know any Monk Evans. And what's the matter with the Indians?"

"They're out raiding." She was wearing a simple house dress with an apron tied around her waist. He said impatiently: "Put on your riding skirt or whatever you want to travel in."

"I'm not going anywhere," she snapped. "If there was any Indian trouble, we'd have heard about it."

"Where's Herb?"

"In the garden. . . ."

Mark didn't wait to hear any more. He didn't know what was the matter with Ruth, and he didn't have time to find out. He strode past her, through the kitchen, and across the back porch. Herb was hoeing in the garden, bent over, working slowly and carefully.

Mark ran toward him, yelling: "Herb, you've got to get to the fort! Indians!"

Jackson straightened, wiping a sleeve across his sweaty face. "Hello, Mark. Haven't seen you . . ." He threw the hoe down. "What's this about Indians?"

Mark told him, adding: "Ruth says she's not going anywhere."

"She'll go," Herb said. "Saddle her horse, will you, son? I'll be with you in a minute."

Jackson wasn't in the house long. By the time Ruth's paint mare and Jackson's horse were saddled, she joined them, tight-lipped and red in the face. They mounted and rode down the

94

slope to the road, Jackson saying: "Hard to tell which way the main band will go. Might come right by here and head into the mountains. They're more mobile than the soldiers, and they know they'll be chased, so they're bound to line out for the mountains somewhere."

He looked back once, then turned his head, his mouth working. "I built well. I'd sure hate to get burned out." He paused, silent until he recovered his self-control, then added: "Indians have my sympathy. They've been mistreated as far back as the first white men had any contact with them. They're like children, talking about how it used to be when there was plenty of game and they could go anywhere whenever they wanted to. They think they can restore the old days, so they start out pillaging and burning, never seeming to realize that tragedy must be the inevitable end."

"I don't have any sympathy for them," Mark said. "They tried to kill me and Bronco this morning. If I hadn't killed three of them, they'd have killed me."

Ruth looked at him, her mouth curling in disbelief. "You killed three of them, did you? Was it Indians? Or flies?

"Ruth," Jackson said sharply.

"Do you believe him?" Ruth demanded. "Do you think it's a likely story that he killed three Indians?"

"Forget it," Mark said, and, after that they rode in silence, Mark hurt and puzzled by Ruth's manner.

They reached the fort at noon. Mark had never seen an Army post, and he was disappointed. No stockade, no blockhouses, just a huddle of buildings, most of them whitewashed or painted white, scattered haphazardly around the parade ground.

"Ruth knows Lieutenant Bolton's wife," Jackson said. "I'll take her there. Missus Bolton will probably have room for her."

Ruth rode on toward the officers' quarters, sitting straight and severe in the saddle and not giving Mark as much as a glance.

Mark saw Bronco with a group of ranchers and reined toward them, trying to put Ruth out of his mind. If that was the way she wanted to treat him, all right, he'd give her the same medicine.

He'd gone out of his way to warn Ruth and her father, and all he'd got for his trouble was a kick in the teeth. Still, no matter how hard he tried to put her out of his mind, a sense of injury rankled, and he was glad to see Bronco grinning at him and motioning for him to get down.

"Here's the old Indian fighter," Bronco said. "He killed three Indians before breakfast, two of 'em before I was out of bed."

A big man with a beard laughed and jolted Bronco with an elbow. "Maybe you had a woman under the blanket with you, and you were so busy you couldn't bother with no Indian fighting."

"Hell, no," Bronco said. "Where would I find a woman? No sir, I was just sawing it off when he goes bang-bang with his six-shooter, and I came up off that bed like I had a Paiute knife in my gut. Mark here says calm-like . . . 'I got two of 'em.'"

They all laughed, and the big man said: "That'll teach you to sleep all day when there's an Indian war going on."

Then Mark was out of the saddle, standing beside Bronco who said: "Mark, meet John Runyan of Triangle R." He was the big man with the beard. His handshake was firm, his voice pleasant when he said: "I'm glad to meet you, son. I've heard Bronco speak of his partner."

Mark went on around the circle, shaking hands with all of them. Some were names he hadn't heard, but two besides John Runyan were familiar to him: Dave Nolan of Rocking Chair, a small, precise man with a carefully trimmed mustache, and Matt Ardell of Bearpaw, a fat man with a scraggly beard and squeaky voice.

Here were the three biggest cowmen in the country—Runyan, Nolan, and Ardell—and none of them looked the part. As he stepped back beside Bronco, the handshaking finished, it seemed to Mark that Bronco looked more like a successful cowman than any of the others.

"You ain't had anything to eat, have you, Mark?" Bronco asked. Mark shook his head, and Bronco said: "Come on over here to the fire. They've got a pot of stew on. I think John cooked it. Don't taste like much, but it's the best they've got to offer."

Runyan laughed. "Not guilty, Bronco. I don't know who cooked it. The hell of it is I went off in such a hurry that I left six pies setting on the shelf that the cook had just pulled out of the oven, but they was too hot to bring." He motioned to one of the men. "Cory, take care of the boy's horse so he can eat."

Mark got a tin plate and cup, filled the plate with stew from the pot, and poured his coffee. Bronco squatted beside him. "So they hadn't been warned."

Mark shook his head. "That damned Monk Evans rode right past their place and didn't say a word. I'm going to bust him on the snout when I see him."

"Aw, forget it. Haven't been here before, have you?"

Mark shook his head. "Doesn't look like a fort to me."

"Well, that's what it is."

Bronco pointed out the three barracks, each of which housed a company; the small buildings for the civilian employees; the quarters for the married soldiers and laundresses, which were on the south edge of the camp; and the officers' quarters, each cottage large enough to hold two families. Mark wondered which one belonged to Lieutenant Bolton, and that brought Ruth back into his mind. Sooner or later he was going to have it out with her. He had a right to know what was wrong.

Bronco was pointing to the big log building, which he said was the commissary storehouse, then the hospital, the post office, the guardhouse, and finally the big cavalry stable with the corrals behind it. "You'll find your sorrel there if you want him," Bronco said.

Matt Ardell drifted over and sat down beside Mark. "The women and kids are scattered all over," he said. "Plenty of room. When we rode in, there were just thirteen soldiers in the whole damned fort. They said we'd have to defend the families, and they handed out some old carbines that wasn't worth a damn. Leastwise, we didn't think they were. Used them old linen cartridges and a hell of a big slug. Well, we went over to the target range and tried 'em out. Hell, we couldn't have hit Shadow Mountain with 'em, let alone a Paiute, so we brought 'em back. We asked if they didn't have anything better. They dug around and found enough Springfields, fifty caliber. That was some better. We allowed we could maybe do some protecting with them."

"You should have fetched your own guns," Bronco said, laughing.

"Well, I guess we was like John and his pies," Ardell said. "We was up north of the lakes when we heard about the trouble, so we lit a shuck for the fort."

Dave Nolan was standing behind Ardell. He said: "The talk is that Captain Bernard will be in tonight with four companies and Robbins's scouts. Some of us are volunteering to go along. How about you, Bronco?"

"Sure, count me 'n' Mark in," Bronco answered. "I've got a score to settle with them red bastards, anyhow."

"The raiding parties they sent out like the one that hit you boys will be trying to catch up with the main band," Nolan went on. "It's my guess they'll head north from Shadow Mountain, and they'll move fast, probably try to reach the Umatilla reservation in hopes they'll pick up some help."

Mark noticed there were other groups of men scattered around, most of them standing beside fires. Jackson had joined one of them. If Bronco saw him, he paid no attention. Several children were playing tag on the parade ground. Two of the boys got into a fight. One of them started to cry, and a woman ran out of one of the officers' cabins, spanked the boy who was crying, and led him back to the cabin by his ear.

"Bernard won't leave any of his men in camp," Ardell was saying, "and we can't figure on the thirteen soldiers who were holding down the fort when we got here to fight off the Paiutes if they get it into their heads to attack."

"They won't," Nolan said. "It's the Army's business about who holds the fort. There won't be any trouble here anyhow."

"How do you know?" Ardell asked.

"The talk is that the Bannock chief, Buffalo Horn, got killed, so I figure the Bannocks have thrown in with the Paiutes, and they'll get Egan to lead them. He's too smart to tackle the fort. He'll head for the mountains."

Ardell shook his head. "With all these women and kids . . ."

"I've got eighteen men who have promised to go," Nolan cut in. "I figure to take our buckaroos and leave the settlers." He paused, his lips squeezing together, then he said with more bitterness than had been in his voice: "Damned funny how many of them there are when they all come out of the hills and show up in one spot like this."

Ardell shrugged. "Nothing to worry about, Dave, as long as they stay in the hills."

The talk ran on, Mark only half listening, for he was thinking of Ruth again and wondering what he had done to antagonize her. His attention wavered back and forth, but he gathered that the Indians had struck hard around Shadow Mountain. Two men who had been surprised in their cabin had had it burned, and they had died in it.

"Which just about happened to us," Bronco said. "I'm still scared when I think about it."

"Then don't," Ardell said. "When I remember all the close shaves I've had since I came to this country, I figure I might as well throw my razor away."

Damn it, Mark thought. *I don't want Ruth sore at me. I've got to see her.*

The men went on, talking about two cowboys who claimed they could handle all the Paiutes and Bannocks in the country single-handed, and had died because they'd refused to run. And how Dave Nolan's ranch had been attacked and his Chinese cook shot and scalped, and Nolan with a Sharps rifle and a belt full of cartridges had held off the Paiutes while his men rode to safety.

"Well, who's getting off the biggest lie now?" a man asked as he walked up.

Monk Evans! For the second time in his life Mark went crazy mad. All he could think of was that the man had ridden within a few yards of the Circle J and hadn't bothered to stop. Only luck and the Lord's mercy had brought the marauding band to the Cross Seven instead of the Circle J.

For a moment Mark sat there, his face turning red, his hands trembling as Ardell said: "No lies, Monk. Hell, this is gospel . . ."

Mark rose and whirled; he hit Evans in the belly as hard as he could. The man was jolted back on his heels, his breath going out of his lungs in an audible whoosh. Then Mark cracked him on the nose and knocked him flat, blood spurting from his nose and running down into his mouth.

Evans muttered an oath, swiped at his mouth, and, lying on his side, raised himself on an elbow. He pulled his gun as he shouted: "No damned kid's gonna belt me like that!"

Evans had his gun out and leveled at Mark, and Mark, not expecting this, was caught flat-footed. He clawed for the .44 in his holster, but he knew he was slow, far too slow.

Mark heard a shot, but it wasn't from Evans's gun. Mark, with his Colt barely clear of leather, saw Evans drop flat on the ground. He said thickly: "Bronco, you . . ." Bronco fired again, the bullet driving through his chest and killing him instantly.

Men ran up, John Runyan among them. He stared at his dead buckaroo, then at Bronco, who still held his smoking gun. Runyan cried out in rage: "What the hell, Curtis?"

"He was fixing to kill the kid," Bronco said flatly. "I ain't one to stand here and let my partner get plugged because he knocked Evans on his butt. The fellow must have been drunk."

"That's right," Nolan said. "The boy knocked him down, and Evans went for his gun. He'd have killed the boy if Curtis hadn't drilled him."

Runyan swung to face Mark. "What'd you hit him for?"

"He warned us, then he went right past the Jackson place without saying anything to them. There was a girl there. She'd have been killed this morning if that bunch of red devils had hit the Jackson place instead of ours."

"That's right," Bronco said. "It wouldn't have taken him five minutes to stop and warn Herb Jackson."

"I wasn't looking for a gunfight," Mark said. "I was just going to give him a beating."

Runyan pulled at his beard, then he muttered: "All right, all right."

"I told you once, Mark," Bronco said in a low voice. "If a man gets on the shoot, accommodate him, but do it first."

Mark nodded, remembering and now fully understanding.

Chapter Twelve

Late in the afternoon Captain Bernard and his four companies arrived at Camp Sherman along with Robbins's scouts. There was a good deal of talk about Buffalo Horn's being killed and the Bannock war party's joining the Paiute malcontents at Shadow Mountain. Old Chief Winnemucca, who hadn't wanted to fight the whites, had made his escape with the help of his son and his daughter Sarah and the Bannock and Paiute bands had united under the Paiute war chief, Egan.

Dave Nolan talked to Bernard and Robbins, telling of his flight north, and reported that he had eighteen volunteers ready to help out. All agreed that Egan, who knew the country, would strike out across Sherman Valley somewhere west of the fort and head for the mountains. It wouldn't take more than a day or two to pick up the Indians' trail and maybe pin them down for a fight. If they could be crushed, the war would be over, and everyone could go home.

Now, watching Bronco, Mark sensed that he was sorry he had promised to go with Nolan. As far as he was concerned, the war was over, and he wanted to get back to the calf branding. But he was committed, and he could not back out. Besides, it was a good thing to have Dave Nolan on his side, for, after the shooting of Monk Evans, it was hard to tell what Bronco's relationship with John Runyan would be.

In spite of Nolan's small size, he was a fighting man and the leader of the cowmen. Runyan, sullenly silent, would follow him. So would Matt Ardell. If Bronco had any worry about what would happen between him and Runyan, he gave Mark no indication of it. But Mark had learned long ago that Bronco was not one to talk about his troubles; he was coldly confident he could handle any difficulty when and if it came. If circumstances compelled him to trade Runyan's friendship for Dave Nolan's, it might be to his advantage, for Nolan was the strongest man in the country.

At dusk Herb Jackson hunted Mark up and drew him away from the others. He asked: "What was the shooting about?"

Mark told him. Jackson kept pushing his spectacles back on his nose as he stared across the parade ground, plainly not seeing the activity that was going on. Bernard would be leaving at dawn, Company K of the 21st Infantry remaining to guard the post on the off chance that the Indians might make an attack to secure guns and ammunition.

"Curtis shouldn't have killed the man," Jackson said finally, as if trying to think this through.

"He'd have killed me if Bronco hadn't," Mark said. "Maybe I shouldn't have hit him."

"No way to know now," Jackson said. "If Evans purposely didn't warn us, hoping the Indians would murder us, then you did right. If he honestly thought we had gone to the fort, I would say you were wrong."

Angry words were on Mark's tongue. He had not suspected Evans of being guilty of anything worse than negligence, but it was the kind of negligence that could not be excused, and Evans had deserved a licking because of it. It had not occurred to Mark that it would go beyond a licking, and all afternoon he had felt guilty for inadvertently bringing on the man's death.

He held the hot words back, staring at Jackson's face in the thinning light as he considered what the man had said. After a time he said: "I don't savvy. Why would Evans want the Indians to murder you?"

"I'm only guessing," Jackson admitted. "Maybe it was Curtis. He won't rest until I'm dead. Every time he sees me, he is reminded of the fact that I'm the only one who knows for sure he murdered Orry Andrews."

"You keep saying it but don't know it," Mark said angrily. "Looks to me like it's only natural Bronco would hate you."

"It's natural, all right," Jackson said. "I haven't told you, Mark, but in spite of Curtis's warning, I kept nosing around on Cross Seven range. Well, now I know, but I haven't decided what I can do about it, the law in the valley being what it is, and Curtis standing in good with men like Runyan and Nolan."

"What do you mean, now that you know?"

"About a month ago I found the bones of a horse," Jackson said. "A mile or so north of Ten Mile Valley close to a game trail. It's my guess that was where Orry left him. Curtis shot him in the back and buried him and the saddle and the rifle. I couldn't find any of those things. The horse was too big for Curtis to move, and he knew the coyotes would soon eat the carcass. Nothing would be left except the bones, and I can't take those into court and prove anything with them."

"You can't prove anything to me, either," Mark said, anger still in him. "The bones of a horse are poor evidence to hang a man."

"To you, perhaps," Jackson said. "Not to me. I told you Orry was my friend. I know he would have stopped at our place and said good bye, but he didn't. If he had met with an accident, say the horse had thrown and killed him, his bones would have been there. So would the rifle and some remnants of the saddle and maybe a belt buckle or his boots. Nothing like that was there, Mark, so they must have been hidden."

Mark could only stand there, staring at Jackson's troubled face in the near darkness and resenting this accusation against a man who was his friend and had saved his life on more than one occasion. He knew that nothing he could say would change Jackson's opinion. He said finally: "You're wrong, Herb." He paused, then added: "What you're trying to say is that Bronco told Evans not to stop at your place?"

"It's possible," Jackson said. "Perhaps he told Evans that we had gone to the fort. Did he have a chance to talk to Evans alone?"

Thinking about it, Mark remembered that Evans had asked for a fresh horse and Bronco had gone to the corral with him to get the animal. Mark nodded and said: "Yes, he had a chance, but it seems to me it was poor odds, thinking the Paiutes would hit your place."

"Not so poor when you remember they almost got you, and we're your closest neighbor. Besides, he probably figured a slim chance was worth trying. From what I heard about the shooting and the way you tell it, Curtis had no reason to fire the second shot that killed Evans unless he wanted to keep him from talking. That's what convinces me."

Mark was silent, not believing any of this, but understanding the futility of arguing. All he could think of was that here were two men who were his friends, both hating each other so much that death was inevitable for one of them at the hands of the other.

"I've had a talk with Ruth," Jackson went on. "She was put out with you because you didn't come to see us all winter."

"I didn't think I'd better," Mark said. "I told Bronco about having Sunday dinner with you, and he said it was all right to see Ruth but not you. I was afraid I'd make trouble for you."

"I knew it was something like that," Jackson said.

"When she rode with me a piece that Sunday, I told her I'd come to see her if Bronco didn't get sore. She said she understood."

"She's a woman," Jackson said gently, "and women forget same as a man. All she remembers is that she wanted you to come and you didn't. I told her she had to talk to you. Tell her what you told me." He motioned vaguely toward the end of the line of houses that made up the officers' quarters. "You watch for her. She'll be along."

Jackson walked off. Mark waited, still not knowing which house belonged to Lieutenant Bolton. If he had known, he would have gone to Ruth instead of her coming to him, and now he wished he'd asked her father. But he hadn't, and, if he moved away, he might miss her.

Presently it was fully dark; the campfires around which the cowmen and settlers were gathered becoming red eyes in the night. Lamps had been lighted in the officers' quarters and the barracks and the big commissary storehouse, and lanterns in the cavalry stables.

The children had been put to bed, their tongues silenced for a few hours, but there was still a good deal of coming and going, shouts, and a little forced laughter from men who were drawing their rations and knew they would see action tomorrow or the following day. None wanted the others to know that he was thinking some Indian might have a bullet with his name on it.

Mark heard Ruth's scream behind him and whirled, drawing his gun. The scream was choked off, and a man cursed as Mark plunged into the darkness. Then he glimpsed them ahead of him, indistinct in the thin light: the man had an arm around Ruth and was holding her in front of him so Mark couldn't shoot.

"Stay back!" the man called. "Stay back or I'll kill her!"

Mark yelled—"Bronco!"—and lunged toward them. Ruth must have bitten the man or scratched his face, because he cursed in pain and flung her aside. Mark fired as he fell against the man, missing him completely.

Ruth screamed a warning. Mark caught a glimpse of the fellow's arm sweeping at him; he felt the sharp stab of a knife in his side, twisting and tearing, then he was shoved back and around. As he fell, he fired again, aimlessly this time.

Vaguely Mark was aware of men shouting and running toward them, of bobbing lanterns and Ruth struggling with the man again. Mark couldn't shoot now, with Ruth so close to his target. He reached out and grabbed the man's leg as he realized Ruth hadn't fled when she'd had a chance but had actually attacked her assailant. If she'd run, Mark would have been stabbed again.

Somehow Mark clung to the leg as it churned back and forth, the man cursing and Ruth hanging on as she bit and kicked and scratched. Then Bronco was there, others running behind him. Bronco jerked the man around, and Ruth, losing her grip on the fellow, fell to her knees.

"What's going on?" someone shouted.

Bronco had slammed the man on his back and had taken the knife from him. Now Bronco's right hand came up and down, and up and down again, the man under him making a strangled, gurgling sound. Someone pulled Bronco off, saying: "You've cut him to pieces, Curtis."

And Runyan: "That's two for you today."

Then someone tipped a lantern so the light fell over the dead man's face. This time it was Nolan who said: "It's that damned saddle tramp, Gentry. He scared two women to death early this spring. We should have hung him then."

Ruth was crying, but she managed to say: "I was walking along here when he grabbed me. Mark? What about Mark?"

Bronco jerked a lantern from someone and put it on the ground beside Mark. "He's bleeding like a stuck hog!" Bronco shouted. "Get the sawbones!"

Ruth's dress had been torn from her throat to her waist. Suddenly she was conscious of it and tried to hold it together. A man took off his coat and gave it to her. Then she was on her knees beside Mark, saying hysterically: "He can't die. God, don't let him die."

Her father came with some of the officers' wives. He said: "A doctor rode in with Bernard's command. Let's carry Mark to the hospital."

The last memory Mark had was that of a woman leading Ruth away, and the thought lingered in his mind that he would not be riding in the morning with Nolan's volunteers. Dave Nolan would have seventeen men instead of the eighteen he had promised Captain Bernard.

Chapter Thirteen

At dawn Mark heard the sounds of Bernard's troops preparing to leave—shouted commands, the piercing tone of the bugle, the clank of metal on metal, the squeal of leather as the men mounted, and finally the fading sound of hoofs on hard ground as they moved out toward the Agency road.

Mark turned his face to the wall, not wanting to see them and forgetting that the light wasn't strong enough for him to see anything. Nolan's volunteers would be with Bernard, Bronco Curtis riding behind Nolan, or maybe beside him, and ahead of John Runyan and Matt Ardell. Not that Matt could see him and not that anyone had told him. He just knew that was where Bronco would be.

Seventeen men instead of eighteen. They'd probably whip the Paiutes without any help from Bernard's command. They were leaving with Nolan commanding them, but they'd return with Bronco running the show. That was Bronco Curtis for you, born to command, born to be big. Maybe Dave Nolan and John Runyan and Matt Ardell didn't know it now, but they'd find out.

Mark's side hurt with steady, infuriating pain. The doctor had dressed his wound hastily the night before, drunk and sullen because he'd been dragged away from a poker game and his bottle. Too, he had known he'd have to ride in the morning with Bernard's command.

The doctor had had a good deal to say about cowboy brawls. If they wanted to fight, he'd complained, they'd better join the

Army and get a bellyful of it. As far as he was concerned, the whole damned country would be better off if the cowboys killed each other and made room for the farmers. Then he'd picked up his black bag and stomped out.

Mark knew he'd be laid up a long time. The doctor had told him that. The wound was a deep one, and he had lost a great deal of blood. Bronco would be sore at him, he thought, with so much work to be done on the Cross Seven this summer. The branding should have been done before now; the building had to be finished before winter, hay cut, wood chopped and hauled, and the big herd that Jacob Smith was sending north to Cross Seven grass would have to be driven onto summer range.

Bronco would be sore at him, all right, and Mark couldn't blame him. Of all the times to be laid up . . . with Bronco needing him the way he did now. It would be the end of their partnership, Mark thought. By the time Lieutenant Bolton's wife brought his breakfast, despair had settled upon him.

Mrs. Bolton was a tall, angular woman who hated the frontier but who hated being separated from her husband even more than she disliked the hardship of living on an isolated Army post. She sat beside Mark trying to get him to eat and to cheer up, but he couldn't eat and he could think of nothing he had cause to be cheerful about. Finally she left, saying that Ruth was all right beyond having had a bad scare the night before.

Then there was nothing for Mark to do but lie there and think about what had happened in the year since the murder of his parents, of the recurring violence that seemed to be the pattern of life in this country. Of Red Malone in Prineville and how Red would have killed him if it hadn't been for Bronco. Of Orry Andrews's disappearance. Of Herb Jackson's hunt for Andrews's body and of himself keeping Bronco from killing Herb. Of the Indian attack and the three Paiutes he had killed. Of Monk Evans's failure to warn the Jacksons and how he had knocked

Monk down and Bronco had killed him. Then the attack on Ruth and his attempt to save her and Bronco's coming in time to kill the man.

Maybe this pattern of violence was not due to the country as much as it was to Bronco Curtis himself. Mark could not forget what Herb Jackson had said, that Bronco was a young man in a hurry, that he was bound to go too far too fast. It was true, Mark knew. Bronco had said he must do in a year what John Runyan and Dave Nolan had done in all the years they had been in this country.

Ruth came later in the day, her face paler than Mark had ever seen it. She sat down beside him and took his hand, trying to smile. She said: "I'm sorry about what happened. I owe you so much. If you hadn't been there . . ."

"It was Bronco," Mark interrupted. "All I did was to get myself stuck with a knife. I'm not much good without Bronco."

"Oh, Mark, it isn't true," she assured. "You're good for an awful lot. Pa says if it wasn't for Curtis, you'd . . ." She stopped and drew her hand from Mark's. "Pa went home this morning. The cow's got to be milked and the chickens fed. Everybody thinks the trouble's over with here in the valley. The Indians will head for the mountains now that the soldiers are after them."

Mark lay there, looking at her and thinking how much he loved her. Maybe she would laugh at him if he told her. She had a right to. He had nothing to offer her. But if he got over this, he would ask her to marry him whether he had anything to offer or not.

He thought how much he had changed in the last year, changed because he had to. As his father used to say, it was root hog or die. He wasn't twenty yet, but he was a man. At least he felt like one. He wasn't afraid any more. Not of the country or his future or anything, really.

For a long time Ruth sat there, staring at her hands, which were folded on her lap. Presently she said: "As soon as you get well enough to be moved, we'll have you brought to our place and I'll nurse you. You'll get well, Mark, but you won't if you go back to the Cross Seven. Curtis will work you to death."

He didn't argue with her. There was too much truth in what she had just said. Bronco had little patience with weakness of any kind, regardless of the cause of the weakness. It was all the more wonder that Bronco had ever put up with him in the first place. But that had been different. No, it wouldn't do for him to go back to Cross Seven and stay in bed, and he couldn't stay here.

Finally he said: "You're good, Ruth. Awfully good."

She bowed her head, refusing to look at him. She said: "I'm sorry about the way I treated you yesterday. I didn't understand. I'm not trying to excuse myself. It was just that I thought you'd come back to see us, and you never did. I guess I was kind of disappointed."

"I wanted to come," he said, "but it might have got your dad into trouble, him feeling the way he does about Bronco."

"I know that now," she said. "Pa told me. I should have known, but all I could think of was that you didn't like my dinner or you didn't like me or something."

"Ruth," he said, "I love you."

He had not intended to say it, but the words came out of him without conscious thought, perhaps driven by the fear that he might lose her. Perhaps he'd never had her, and a man couldn't lose something he'd never had, but she had been angry at him because he hadn't returned after that Sunday last fall, and he couldn't let her think it was due to anything she had done or said or that she was in any way to blame.

So he said the words he had not intended to say at this time, and he was not prepared for the effect it had upon her. She rose and, bending over him, kissed him on the lips. Then she fled from the room, and he was alone with only the whitewashed walls of the room for company, and the memory of her kiss.

After that, Mrs. Bolton took care of Mark; she told him that Ruth had returned to the Circle J. A few days later two wounded men from the battle at Silver Creek were brought in, one from Company L and one from Company G, and Mark heard the story of how Bernard had surprised the Indians on the Sunday morning after he'd left the fort and had beaten them. They had fled northward toward the John Day country, the war chief, Egan, badly wounded.

General Howard arrived at the fort with his staff and went on to help Bernard. Nolan's volunteers returned, and Bronco came at once to see Mark. He stood looking down at Mark, dirty, stubble-faced, big, and straight-backed, and proud of himself and what he had done.

"We sure gave 'em hell, boy," he said. "They had us outnumbered 'bout ten to one, looked to me like, but we whipped 'em. Wish you could have had some of the fun."

"Yeah, so do I," Mark said.

"How do you feel?" Bronco asked.

"Terrible," Mark said. "I won't be doing any work for a while, I guess."

"We'll get it done," Bronco assured him. "I'm going to hire some hands. Runyan's promised to send his carpenters in a few days, and I'm going to get the lumber hauled right away. Things will quiet down now, and we'll get some work done."

He stood twirling his hat in his hands, awkward and uncertain about what to say, then he blurted: "Missus Bolton, she says the Jackson girl told her she was taking you to her place soon as you can travel."

"I guess so," Mark said. "I won't be any good on the Cross Seven for a long time. Just be in your way."

Bronco cleared his throat. "You sweet on the girl?"

Mark resented the question. It was none of Bronco's business. But Mark had neither the strength nor desire to argue, so he said—"Yes."—and let it go at that.

"Don't blame you," Bronco said. "She's as purty as a new red-wheeled buggy. Marry her, boy, and fetch her to Cross Seven. We'll be proud of the spread and proud of her. We'll do some entertaining soon as we get squared around. With Jacob Smith backing us, we'll have Runyan and Nolan and Ardell coming to us. You'll see."

Then Bronco shook his head and grinned. "By God, Mark, you look like hell. Take it easy. You hear?"

He nodded, clapped his hat on his head, and strode out.

Dave Nolan dropped in to see Mark, and later in the day Matt Ardell came. For some reason Mark liked this fat man with the scraggly beard and squeaky voice better than either Runyan or Nolan.

"Tell me about Bronco," Mark said. "He's not one to brag."

"He had plenty of reason to brag," Ardell said. "He just kind of took over, and damned if Nolan didn't let him. We were with Robbins's scouts, you know, supposed to get upstream from the Indian camp and start the ruckus. We done it, all right, with Bronco leading us along with Nolan. The soldiers came in on the other side, and all hell started to pop, the bugle tooting and the guns going off, and them red bastards half naked and fighting like they was old Nick hisself."

Ardell laughed. "Never seen nothing like it and I hope I never do again. Egan and Robbins tied into each other, and Egan got wounded. More'n once. Bronco gave him one bullet anyhow. He was all over the place, Bronco was. We went piling through the camp twice. Hard to tell how many the Indians lost, but it was considerable."

Ardell paused and scratched the bald spot on his head. "The next day the cavalry got on the Indians' tail. We figured they didn't need us no more, so we came back. Funny thing. Bronco was riding in front with Nolan, or ahead of him part of the time, and anybody watching would have figured he was the big cheese."

Mark had told himself it would be like that. From now on everybody in the country would hear about Bronco Curtis, perhaps even Jacob Smith a thousand miles away.

"Sorry you're laid up like this," Ardell said. "I was talking to Missus Bolton. She said Gentry gave you a bad one. He was no good. We knew it and told him to leave the country, but nobody ever got around to making it stick."

He got up, giving his trousers a tug upward, but they immediately slipped back below his round belly. "Son," Ardell said, "you're Bronco's friend, and that's good. A man needs friends. Trouble is Bronco don't want to take time to grow. We all oughta take a little time, just for other men to watch it happen if there ain't no other reason. Maybe you can slow him up, huh? Be good for him if you could."

"I'll try," Mark said, thinking how close Ardell had come to saying the same thing Herb Jackson had said.

The next day the settlers and cowmen were gone, leaving only the wounded and a skeleton force in the fort. Mark resented his weakness and fought with his impatience as he fought with Mrs. Bolton, who spent most of her time with him, but it was July before she let him go in an ambulance to the Circle J, weak and thin and constantly tired and very conscious of the fact that he owed his life to Mrs. Bolton.

Later, through the hot days of July, he realized he owed a debt to Ruth and her father, too, and he was depressed by the knowledge that life was filled with obligations and a man couldn't live long enough to repay them. Then he wondered if Bronco was ever aware that he owed anything to anybody. Mark doubted that he was, for Bronco Curtis was the kind of man who wove the pattern of his own destiny.

Chapter Fourteen

Through the weeks that Mark stayed at the Circle J, his relationship with Ruth was one of restraint on his part and of disappointment on hers. At least he sensed that was her feeling, for he often caught her looking at him when his attention had been fixed on something else. Then when she knew he was looking at her, she would glance away quickly, but he always felt he caught a look of expectancy in her face, as if she hoped he would tell her again that he loved her.

But he couldn't. He had told her once when he had not intended to, but now, mired down by physical weakness, he realized what poor husband material he was. He wasn't sure whether he was boy or man; he wasn't sure whether he could count on any of the promises Bronco Curtis had made. So he remained silent.

He regained his strength slowly, doing a few chores at first, working in the garden or helping Jackson with his hay. Once his side tore open and started to bleed again. Worried, Ruth insisted that he go back to bed. She stopped the bleeding with cobwebs and told him hotly that he never would get well if he drove himself the way he had been.

"The doctor did a poor job," Jackson said, "but it's what you can expect from a poor doctor."

"I'm not built to enjoy being an invalid," Mark said. "I've been sponging off you folks too long now."

They were sitting on the front porch at dusk, the haying finished and Herb Jackson feeling that his work was caught up for the first time since the Indian trouble.

Ruth said—"Sponging."—as if it were an ugly word. "Oh, Mark, you fool." She flounced into the house, and they heard her banging dishes in the kitchen.

Jackson laughed softly as he filled his pipe. "By nature youth is impatient," he said, "and Ruth is very young." He lighted his pipe and pulled on it, then took it out of his mouth. "The crossing from youth to manhood or womanhood is a trying time in any human being's life. It's filled with danger and sometimes with suffering, and there is invariably a feeling that time drags and the waiting will never pass."

He glanced at Mark, who sat beside him. "You know, many grown people never make the crossing, even though they believe they have. They never think or feel like adults, or take an adult's responsibility. I think the test is whether a man learns to act by his own standards of morality or whether he simply follows someone else's. I suspect that is why men join the Army. They can quit thinking for themselves. All they have to do is to follow orders."

Mark was silent, for he knew what Jackson was driving at. He was asking, in his kindly, indirect way, whether Mark had reached the place where he could strike out on his own, or whether he would return to the Cross Seven and pick up with Bronco Curtis where he had left off. Mark wasn't sure himself, but he had thought about it and knew he wasn't ready yet to come to a decision.

"I told Ruth once that I loved her," Mark said. "I still do. I always will, but I don't have anything. I can't ask her to marry me, Herb."

Jackson stared across the valley, the far rims lost in the twilight. He said: "You haven't made the crossing yet, and I'm not sure Ruth has. You're like a hothouse plant that was suddenly transplanted into a world of hot sunny days and frosty nights. It's to your credit that you have survived as well as you have. You'll make the crossing, but not until you've made your own decision about Bronco Curtis and how you feel about him."

"You forget something," Mark said. "I owe my life to him." Silence then, except for the raucous cry of some night bird wheeling across the sky. Jackson cradled the pipe in his hand, still staring at the horizon that was being brought closer by the night.

Finally Jackson said: "Mark, you will disagree with me, but I have a belief that it is not a man's deeds that are important. Rather, it is the motive behind the deed. True, Curtis saved your life when this Red Malone would undoubtedly have killed you, but you don't know why he did it. Certainly not from any affection for you, because he hardly knew you. Someday you will understand his motive, and then you will know what to do."

Ruth came out of the house. She sat down beside Mark and took his hand. She said: "I'm sorry about my temper. I've got plenty of it. I just didn't want to hear you talking about sponging off us."

After that they talked about the Indian war and how the Paiutes had been driven north and Egan murdered by an Umatilla, who cut off his head and hands and brought them to the Army camp. And of the new town, Scott City, which had been started on the Agency road a few miles southwest of Camp Sherman, and about the big herd Jacob Smith had sent north to Cross Seven range and the fine house Bronco Curtis had built.

"It's like I told you once before about Curtis," Jackson said. "Here's a young man in a hurry. When Ruth and I came here, I loved this country. It was big and open and the way God gave it to man. A lot of families could have made a living here, but it wasn't to be that way, not with the cowmen here. Runyan, Nolan, and Ardell, and then Curtis. As they build up their herds, they need more grass, and, as they need more grass, they push at us who are on the fringe of their range. In time there will be more killings, just as Orry Andrews was killed. What most of us respect as law means nothing to them."

His voice was filled with bitterness, as it always was when he spoke of Andrews. Now he said with even more bitterness: "I'm a tortured soul. I never knew what it was to live in hell until Curtis came. Now I can't forget that I must bring Curtis to justice, but I don't know how to do it. I tell myself I should hide in the timber and murder Curtis the way he killed Orry, but I can't do it. Someday I'll ride to Cañon City and tell the sheriff, even though I know it won't do any good."

"Don't, Pa," Ruth said softly. "You just make yourself suffer."

"I know, I know," he said, "but how can I help it?"

Mark didn't answer. Neither did Ruth. There was no answer, and both of them knew it.

As soon as Mark was strong enough, he began cutting the winter's supply of wood. His side hurt, but it didn't tear open again. In spite of Ruth's protests, he kept at it, working a little longer each day. Sometimes Jackson helped him, but on other days he left after breakfast and was gone all day, giving neither Ruth nor Mark any hint where he was going. Mark was convinced he was searching for Orry Andrews's grave. Finding the skeleton of the horse had not been enough.

"Can't you keep Herb at home?" Mark asked Ruth. "If he doesn't stay off Cross Seven range, Bronco will kill him."

She shook her head, her face filled with misery. "Nothing I can do. Nothing anyone can do, once Pa gets his head set."

Mark knew she was right, so he said nothing to Jackson until one evening when he came home with a bullet hole in the crown of his hat, a shallow scalp wound, and a headache. Mark couldn't remain silent any longer. He burst out: "Herb, you're going to get yourself killed. Stay off Cross Seven range."

"I wish I could, but I can't," Jackson said.

"Who shot you?"

"I don't know. I'd just topped a ridge when someone cut loose at me from down in the timber. He fired three times and the third one tagged me." He put a hand on Mark's shoulder. "Promise me something. If I don't come back someday, will you look out for Ruth?"

Mark nodded, his eyes on the man's worried face. "You know I will, Herb."

"That makes me feel better." Jackson dropped his hand and turned away. "You think I'm crazy, and maybe I am, but if law is to be anything more than theory to me, and if friendship is anything more than a whim, then I've got to see that Curtis pays for Orry's murder."

After that Mark wondered if Jackson actually sought death and would welcome it. As he had said, he was a tortured soul. Bringing Bronco to justice had become an obsession with Jackson; he was a machine set to do something, and he could not help himself.

Mark had his own problem, and he thought about it a great deal. He couldn't stay here. Sooner or later he must return to Cross Seven. Neither Jackson nor Ruth would understand, but it was something he had to do. Bronco had made a promise of partnership, and it was the only chance Mark had of coming to Ruth with anything except empty hands. Still, he didn't want to go, and he kept putting it off until a Sunday afternoon in September when a rider coming from the Cross Seven turned off the Agency road and came up the slope to the Jackson house.

Mark was sitting on the front porch with Ruth and Jackson, dinner finished, the dishes washed and dried. Mark saw Jackson stiffen, his hands clutching the arms of his rocking chair. "Know him, Herb?" Mark asked.

"I've seen him in Scott City," Jackson said. "He's Curtis's *segundo*. Came north with the Smith herd, I've been told."

Mark went into the house, buckled his gun belt around him, and returned to the porch. He was standing on the ground in front of the house when the rider reined up and lifted his hat to Ruth, then said—"Howdy."—to Jackson, and nodded at Mark.

Jackson said—"Howdy."—and waited, giving the man no invitation to step down. He was a small, knot-headed man, his face weather-bronzed, his expression one of controlled hostility. He wore a gun, but he showed no intention of using it. He folded his hands over the saddle horn, his gaze moving from Jackson to Mark as if sizing them up. He had not come for trouble, Mark thought, and so relaxed.

"My name's Gene Flagler," the man said. "I ride for Cross Seven. You're Herb Jackson?"

"I'm Jackson." Jackson rose and stepped off the porch. "Anything I can do for you?"

"I took a shot at you the other day," Flagler said. "You had orders to stay off Cross Seven range. Next time I'll aim an inch or two lower. But that ain't what I came for. Next year Jacob Smith will send another herd north. Cross Seven will need more grass, so we'll be pushing over the hills. Bronco will buy you out if you want to sell."

It was a threat as well as an offer, but, if Jackson realized it, he gave no sign. He said: "I'm not selling."

Flagler shrugged. "Your choice." He looked at Mark. "You're the Kelton kid, I reckon. Bronco says to come home."

Mark hesitated, feeling Jackson's and Ruth's eyes on him, and sensing Flagler's indifference. But Mark had no doubt about what this was. Bronco Curtis could not come to Circle J himself, so he had sent Flagler. Mark's choice was clear. He could go now or make a complete break with Bronco. But he couldn't leave Bronco. Not yet, anyway.

"I'll be there," Mark said, and heard Ruth gasp behind him.

Flagler nodded. "I'll tell Bronco," he said, and rode away.

When Mark turned to Ruth, she was staring at him as if she could not believe what she had heard. He went to her and took her hands. He said: "Someday I'm going to ask you to marry me, but I've got to have something before I do."

"You think you'll get it from Bronco Curtis?" she demanded.

"We're partners," Mark said.

"You mean he called you that." Her lips curled in disdain. "You worked for him almost a year, and he never gave you anything."

"He was getting started," Mark said. "He didn't have any money for himself or me."

"He had money to gamble at the fort," she said, "and money to buy whiskey, but none to pay you."

Mark glanced at Jackson, who nodded. "I heard it during the Indian trouble. Missus Bolton had heard it, too. She told Ruth."

Bronco was older, Mark thought, and maybe he had to have a little entertainment. Besides, it was Bronco's money. Mark said: "I've got to go."

"Go ahead," she said. "I don't care. Just don't come back. I've waited and waited, but I'm not going to keep on waiting."

She tried to break free from his grasp, but he held her and made her face him. "I'll come back, and I've got a right to ask you to wait a little longer. Don't marry anyone else."

"Who is there to marry in a god-forsaken country like this?" she said bitterly. "Nobody but you, and you won't have me."

"I'll have you and I want you," he said, "but this isn't the time."

"And it never will be," she flung at him. "Let me go."

She started to cry. He said—"Don't."—and kissed her, but she turned her head, so he caught only a corner of her mouth, and the instant she got her hands free, she ran into the house, stumbling over the threshold and almost falling.

When Mark turned, he saw that Jackson had crossed the yard to the corral. There, Jackson waited, saying nothing until

Mark had saddled his sorrel. Then Mark held out his hand. He expected a lecture about holding his own standard of morality and not following Bronco's, but Jackson said nothing. He simply gave Mark's hand a firm shake and, dropping it, stepped back.

Mark swung into the saddle and looked down at Jackson, who was pushing his iron-rimmed spectacles back on his nose. He sensed that the man hated to see him go as much as Ruth did, or as much as he hated to go himself.

"You can't thank people for saving your life," Mark said, "but I'd like . . ."

"Don't try," Jackson said. "And don't let what Ruth said keep you away, either."

"I'll be back," Mark said, and rode away.

When he reached the Agency road and turned toward Cross Seven, he looked back once, but he did not see either Ruth or her father. He went on, his sense of loss almost as great as when his parents were killed. But there was a difference. This was something he had done himself.

Chapter Fifteen

Mark found it hard to believe his eyes as he rode through the meadows past the great stacks of hay toward the new Cross Seven buildings. Bronco had the big ranch house he had dreamed about, a long, two-story building that had been painted white. It stood downstream from the old cabin and farther back on the ridge. There was a bunkhouse and there was a cook shack, but no new barn. Andrews's slab shed would have to do for another winter.

Mark unsaddled and let his sorrel into the corral, then he stood motionlessly, staring at the sprawling house, a strange, almost grotesque symbol of Bronco Curtis's ambition. Mark wondered where the money had come from to build the house, if Jacob Smith had loaned him that much. Mark wondered, too, if Bronco was happy now that he had the buildings he wanted. Probably not, he thought, for Bronco was a man whose accomplishments would never catch up with his ambitions.

A lanky buckaroo appeared from the slab shed. He looked Mark over coldly, then he said arrogantly: "You've got a hell of a lot of gall, kid. Not many saddle tramps would throw their horses into a Cross Seven corral without opening their mugs about it."

Mark moved toward the cowboy, anger touched off by the man's words. It was too much to be jumped by a Johnny-come-lately after what he had gone through last winter. He said: "Go to hell."

"Get that sorrel out of there," the buckaroo said.

Mark stopped, watching the other man walk toward him on the balls of his feet, hands fisted at his sides, cocky and belligerent. Now that he was close, Mark saw that the fellow wasn't much older than he was. Perhaps he had to prove something to Bronco and the crew, or maybe he thought Mark would be easy to handle. Whatever his motives were, he was bent on making trouble.

A step away, the cowboy said: "Get that horse out of there, or I'll . . ."

Mark hit him in the stomach, a slamming blow that drove his breath out of him and doubled him up. For a moment he stood hugging his middle, completely helpless as he strained for breath. Mark hit him on the chin, knocking him flat on his back. He was out cold, his head in a fresh pile of horse manure.

Men rushed out of the bunkhouse, Gene Flagler in the lead. One of them yelled: "Hey, look what he done to Andy!"

"Tote him over to the horse trough and stick his head in," Flagler said. He nodded at Mark. "Come on. Bronco will want to see you."

"He ought to," Mark said. "He sent for me, didn't he?"

"Uhn-huh." Flagler glanced sideways at Mark. "Know who you just tangled with?"

"No. I don't care much, either. He was aiming to run me off the ranch."

"He's Andy Wheeling, Jacob Smith's nephew."

"I still don't care. This is Bronco's spread, and I'm supposed to be his partner."

"Partner?" Flagler's thin lips made a tight grin. "Well, kid, you oughta know one thing. There's room for just one partner on Cross Seven, and his name is Jacob Smith."

They reached the front porch, Flagler calling: "Bronco, the kid's here!"

Bronco stepped through the door, his hand extended. "By God, Mark, it's good to see you." He pumped Mark's hand, then slapped him on the back. "I thought you'd moved in with the Jacksons."

Bronco was thinner than he'd been the last time Mark had seen him, his cheek bones threatening to break through the skin of his face, which had more of a hawk-like look about it than ever. Mark said: "I was pretty sick."

"You look all right now. We can use another good man, eh, Gene?"

"A good man," Flagler agreed, "but I ain't sure about this hairpin. He just knocked Andy colder'n a side of bacon."

"That so?"

Bronco's questioning eyes met Mark's, and suddenly Mark was aware that he stood as tall as Bronco. The knowledge filled him with a heady kind of satisfaction. He lacked Bronco's breadth of shoulders, but that would come with time.

"He didn't ask who I was," Mark said. "He just told me to get my horse out of the corral. Who's got a better right to be here than I have, Bronco?"

"Nobody," Bronco said quickly. "You savvy that, Gene?"

Flagler shrugged. "Sure, I savvy. I likewise savvy that Jacob Smith ain't gonna cotton to the idea of having his nephew kicked around."

"I don't care if Andy's Jacob Smith's grandma," Bronco said hotly. "I ain't gonna baby him no more'n anybody else. You savvy that?" Flagler shrugged again and was silent. "Come on, Mark, I want you to meet the crew. You'll sleep here in the house and eat with me, but you'd best get acquainted with the boys."

He led the way to the bunkhouse, Mark keeping step with him, Flagler having to trot to keep up, his ugly face turned uglier by the scowl that lined his forehead and laid his lips thinly against his yellow teeth and curled his mouth downward at the corners. Mark had a hunch what the crew would be like before he met them, and he was right. They were a salty bunch, not at all like the buckaroos Mark had met at the fort who rode for Runyan or Nolan or Matt Ardell.

They shook hands with Mark because they had to, greeting him sullenly and making it plain that he was an outsider and would remain an outsider. Andy Wheeling, sitting on his bunk with his left hand held to his chin where Mark had hit him, shook hands without getting up, his eyes not meeting Mark's.

"This boy's my partner," Bronco said, his hand on Mark's shoulder. "I wouldn't be here if it wasn't for him. He beefed three Paiutes last June. Laid two of 'em out right in front of the cabin and the other one by the corral." He threw a glance at Andy Wheeling. "Don't none of you make the mistake of trying to make him think he ain't welcome on Cross Seven."

He went out, Mark following. Bronco took him to the cook shack and introduced him to the Chinese cook, Lee Sam, who bowed and grinned blandly and said: "Belly good."

Outside Bronco laughed. "That's about all the English he knows. If the boys holler about what's on the table, he just grins and says . . . 'Belly good glub.' It usually is, too."

Bronco was silent until they were inside the house. Then he pointed at the cavernous stone fireplace at one end of the living room, the Cross Seven brand burned into the mantle. "The carpenters from Triangle R built the house, but Jacob Smith sent up a rock man to build the fireplace. He done a hell of a good job, too. I've ordered some furniture from The Dalles, which ought to be in before snow flies. After I get back from Winnemucca, I'm going to have a house warming and invite Runyan, Nolan, and Ardell. They'll come, all right." He laughed. "They'd be afraid not to, with Jacob Smith backing me."

Bronco motioned at the furniture in the room. "Not much, is it? Hell, I couldn't find nothing for sale at the fort or in Scott City. I got some beds and a couple of pine bureaus.

The old leather couch over yonder and a chair. That's about all. I even had to move up the stove from the cabin until I can get a new one."

From the back of the house a woman called: "Supper's ready, Bronco!"

"I didn't tell you I had a woman, did I?" Bronco asked. "Well, I have, and she's a good one. Looks after me like a wife would. Better'n a wife, the way I see it. I can send her packing when I get tired of her and get me a new one."

Bronco led the way into the dining room. He nodded at the woman standing at the end of the table. "Sharon, meet Mark Kelton. He'll be living with us from now on. Mark, this is Sharon Sanders."

She stepped around the table to shake hands with him. "I've often heard Bronco speak of you, Mark," she said. "I'm glad you're here. I'll set another plate for you. I didn't know you were coming, but there's plenty."

She brought a plate and silverware from the kitchen, and motioned for him to pull up one of the benches that Andrews had left in the cabin. "We ain't real fancy yet, Mark," she said, "but Bronco says we will be before winter."

Bronco had sat down and was already eating with his usual noise and gusto. Sharon sighed and grimaced at Mark. "I don't guess that fancy dining-room furniture will change Bronco's eating habits."

"You do your eating and I'll do mine," Bronco said harshly.

"Yes, Bronco," she said, and sat down at the opposite end of the table from him.

She was about twenty-five, Mark judged, a blonde woman with blue eyes, a little too plump, but good-looking enough. Her features were far from regular; her nose was fat, her lips full, her chin square, but Mark, glancing at her as she ate, could not deny that she was a lusty, attractive woman.

Several times during the meal Mark's eyes met Sharon's, and she always smiled as if wanting to make him feel at home. Presently he realized she was measuring him just as he was measuring her. There was a quality about her, perhaps the bold way her eyes met his, that made him feel she was as predatory in her way as Bronco was in his.

Bronco finished eating, belched loudly, and taking a cigar from his vest pocket, bit off the end, and lit it. "A little different from the way it was last June, ain't it, Mark?" he asked.

"Quite a little different," Mark said. "At least the cooking's improved."

Sharon smiled appreciatively. "Thank you, Mark. The only compliment I ever get from Bronco is the way he gobbles up everything I set in front of him."

Bronco rose, his cigar tucked into one corner of his mouth. "I pay you to keep house. Compliments wasn't part of the bargain."

Bronco stalked into the front room. Sharon rose, frowning. "It's a short ride from the time you're born to the time you die, Mark. I figure a person's entitled to enjoy the ride."

Sharon wouldn't last the winter, Mark thought as he left the dining room. He sensed a discord between her and Bronco. In fact, it seemed there was no harmony anywhere on Cross Seven. There was an end to even Bronco's talents for shaping other people to serve his needs.

Bronco stood with his back to the fireplace, pulling hard on his cigar. He said: "Mark, I'm sure glad to have you home. A lot of work to be done this fall. You see the hay we got stacked?"

Mark nodded. "Looked like a good crop."

"You bet it's a good crop," Bronco said. "We'll get through any kind of a winter. Last spring you said we couldn't do as good with a big herd of cows at calving time as we did with the shirt tailful we had?"

"I remember," Mark said.

"Well, we will. You'll see. I aim to satisfy Jacob Smith so he'll send another herd north. That Gene Flagler has got more cow savvy than any man I ever met."

"Bronco," Mark said, "you're making a mistake."

Bronco bristled. "What are you driving at?"

"That's Jacob Smith's crew out there, isn't it? And Smith's cook." Mark motioned toward the dining room. "Even Sharon Sanders was Smith's woman, wasn't she?"

Bronco took the cigar out of his mouth. "Still sharp as a tack, ain't you?" He grinned. "You're right, but it ain't a mistake. They'll work for me, every damned one of 'em, and that includes Sharon. I had to lick hell out of two of the boys, but now they know who's boss. No, it ain't no mistake. We're on our way, Mark. Don't you ever doubt it."

Mark sat down on the leather couch. "Flagler offered to buy Herb Jackson out. He said you'd be pushing over the hills next summer."

"We will," Bronco said. "Jackson can sell this fall and get something out of his place, or nothing when we need his grass. It's up to him." Bronco turned the cigar with his fingers, staring at it. "I'm sorry if Ruth gets hurt, but as far as Jackson's concerned, I'll be happy to bust him flat, and you know why."

"Bronco." Mark leaned forward. "I'm going to marry Ruth."

"I'm glad," Bronco said. "Damned glad. I told you before. Fetch her here. She'll be queen of the place. Cross Seven needs a woman. A good woman, not that whore I've got in the kitchen. Hell, I don't know why I ever fetched her from Winnemucca."

"Ruth won't come," Mark said. "Not with you and Herb feeling like you do."

"Well, that's up to her. I'd do anything for Ruth and you, but nothing for her father."

"I'd like my wages," Mark said. "I've got some coming from the time we started here until June."

"Wages?" Bronco was affronted. "What the hell's the matter with you? You know we're partners. I don't have money for wages. You stick with me, and one of these days we'll split the biggest damned melon you ever seen."

"You've got money to buy furniture," Mark said. "And to throw away gambling and drinking at the fort. I figure you've got it for me, too."

"I need furniture to make a show," Bronco said patiently. "It's important. You know that. I told you I'll be having an open house. What would it be like this way? As for drinking and gambling, I was always ahead of the game. I never lost a cent. I don't pay myself wages, so you can't expect any."

Herb Jackson and Ruth had been right, Mark thought bitterly. He had worked for nothing. When the time came to split the melon, there wouldn't be any melon.

Bronco was done talking. He picked up a lamp and walked toward the stairs, saying: "We'd best roll in. Got a lot of work to do. I'm gonna drain the tulle swamp and burn it off. Got to have more hay land."

Mark followed him up the stairs, the strong smell of new pine lumber a pleasant fragrance. Bronco opened a door and, going into the room, set the lamp on a box. The bed was the only other piece of furniture in the room. "You can see for yourself what we need." Mark nodded. Bronco stepped back into the hall and closed the door.

Mark pulled off his boots and stretched out on the bed. He asked himself if he should go on working for Bronco for nothing? Did he still owe Bronco anything, or had he paid whatever debt he had once owed? If he left, what would he do? There would be no work in the valley after fall roundup. The big outfits to the south would be cutting down the size of their crews instead of taking on new hands.

As he thought about it, he became angry. What did Bronco expect of him? When you got right down to it, Bronco owed him a hell of a lot more than he owed Bronco. But that didn't make any difference. Not to Bronco. It boiled down to a proposition of having a place to work for his keep, no more and no less.

He got up and took off his shirt and pants, then paced around the room, too restless to sleep. Presently he sat down on the bed again, his head in his hands. He heard the door open and looked up as Sharon slipped into the room, wearing a lacey robe over her nightgown.

She put a finger to her lips, came to the bed, and sat down beside him and slipped an arm around him. He felt the pressure of her breasts as she put her face close to his. She said softly: "I can't stay long. If Bronco knew I was in here, he'd cut my heart out. You're a good, decent kid, Mark, too decent to throw in with Bronco. Get out while you can. You'll only have trouble if you stay."

She turned his face to her and kissed him on the lips, then rose and left the room. Staring at the closed door, he knew she was right. He'd have to leave on her account if for no other reason.

That night he had trouble sleeping.

Chapter Sixteen

Apparently it never occurred to Bronco that Mark might not have fully recovered from his wound or that his side still could be bothering him. He got Mark up at dawn the first morning he was back on Cross Seven. They ate breakfast together in the kitchen, with Sharon serving them and looking, Mark thought, as bright and shiny as a newly minted dollar.

Sharon didn't miss a chance to touch him when she brought something to the table, or to lean over him when she poured his coffee so that he felt the pressure of her big breasts. Mark was stirred by her, but he was uneasy, too. He refused to look at her, although she smiled warmly at him. He rose and went out through the back door as soon as he finished eating, but Bronco didn't come for a time.

Pausing on the porch, Mark heard Bronco say: "You try getting into bed with that kid and I'll run you back to Nevada and slap your butt every jump you make."

She laughed at him. "You'll slap my butt, all right. I guess you like the feel of it. You sure never miss a chance."

"I'm not joshing. You let him alone."

"He's a nice-looking boy, and I like him," Sharon said. "In case you've forgot, our deal didn't include you telling me who I can get in bed with and who I can't. As far as Mark's concerned, that's between him and me."

Mark tiptoed off the porch, not wanting to hear any more. He was excited by the thought that Sharon liked him, that he probably wouldn't even have to ask her to go to bed with him, then he had a weird feeling that Ruth was standing beside him, and he was ashamed.

Bronco caught up with him, breathing hard and red in the face. He said: "You stay away from that bitch. She won't do nothing for you but give you a dose. I never seen a woman like her. She's just like a man with a good-looking girl in the house."

Mark said nothing. He wondered whether Bronco was genuinely concerned about him, or whether he was jealous. Probably the latter, he thought, and, glancing sideways at Bronco's dark face, honed down by hard work until his features seemed to be all sharp points and angles, he told himself that Bronco was not genuinely concerned about anything or anybody but the Cross Seven and himself.

That morning Bronco put Mark to cleaning out the corrals. The crew saddled up and rode out with Bronco, all of them ignoring Mark except Andy Wheeling, who yelled: "Get to work, buckaroo! Lean on that fork handle." Gene Flagler spoke sharply to him, and Wheeling grinned and nodded.

From that day on nothing was the same between Mark and Bronco. The old relationship was gone. The spring before Mark had been a good enough hand to work cattle with Bronco, but now he was a laborer, a chore boy. The crew pretended he didn't exist, the lone exception being Andy Wheeling who hoorawed him every chance he had.

Mark couldn't quite put his finger on the trouble between him and Bronco. Maybe it wasn't trouble at all, maybe it was just that Bronco was so immersed in his dreams and schemes that he had no time for Mark. Even on the few occasions when the two of them were together in the ranch house, Bronco would sit in morose silence in front of the fireplace, pulling on his cigar, his forehead puckered in thought.

Mark had expected to ride on fall roundup, but, no, the tulle swamp must be drained or there was firewood to chop for Lee Sam or Sharon, or wood to be hauled from the ridge above the house, where it had been cut the previous summer. At times Mark had the feeling Bronco would be relieved if he pulled out, but that didn't make sense. He wouldn't have sent Gene Flagler to the Circle J to bring him back if that was the way he felt.

More than once Mark made up his mind to leave, but there was always that will-o-the-wisp promise Bronco had made about a partnership, and, if Mark rode out, there would be a final breaking between them. If he stayed, something might come of it. But when he thought about it, he knew it would be years, and he couldn't wait. So he stayed, teetering in indecision and thinking that each day would be his last, yet nothing happened that forced a decision.

On the afternoon before Bronco was to start south with the little jag of steers that was to go with the Triangle R herd to Winnemucca, Sharon came out of the house and walked to where Mark was sawing wood. It was an unseasonably hot day for so late in the year, and Sharon's face was red and sweaty from standing over the kitchen stove.

"You're working too hard, honey," Sharon said as she sat down on the chopping block. "You'll never get paid, but I guess you know that."

Mark kept sawing until he finished the cut and the block at the end of the log dropped into the pile of sawdust. Then he took off his hat, wiped his forehead with his sleeve, and sat down beside her. "How do you know?" he asked.

She shrugged. "Because I know Bronco Curtis, and I knew Jacob Smith before I knew Bronco. They're a lot alike, using other people to get where they want to be, or using somebody for their pleasure like Jacob done with me. When he got tired of me, he threw me to Bronco. It's the same as tossing a bone from the table to a hungry dog. I'm the bone. Bronco's the dog. He's hungry, honey. Believe me, he's so damned hungry he'll eat anything that's in front of him."

Sharon had been very careful to appear indifferent to Mark after that first morning, probably because she was afraid of Bronco, but now she sat with her knees tucked under her chin, her arms around her legs, her eyes on Mark. Again he felt the throbbing sense of excitement, then the uneasiness, and he looked away from her.

"Bronco's always talked about a partnership," Mark said. "Why do you think he won't pay me?"

"Sure, it was a partnership as long as he needed you, honey," she said. "Well, he don't need you now. You can stay here as long as you're willing to work for your keep. Just don't expect nothing more."

Mark sat staring at the old cabin that had been his and Bronco's home last winter, then he shifted his gaze to the brush along the creek where the Paiutes had hidden. He thought about how hard he and Bronco had worked at calving time, and about the killing of Monk Evans, and about how Gentry had attacked Ruth and wounded him and then been killed by Bronco. It was hard to believe that his relationship with Bronco meant so little, yet he knew it was true. He just hadn't wanted to believe it, so he had come back to the Cross Seven, hoping for something that he hadn't found.

"You're almost twenty, aren't you?" Sharon asked. He nodded, and she went on: "You're a man. Man enough to get married, I'd say from the looks of you. Bronco says you're in love with the Jackson girl. Marry her, honey. Don't wait. It's a short ride from birth to death. Make it a good ride, Mark."

"I don't have anything," he said miserably. "That's why I've been waiting."

"You're a fool," Sharon said impatiently. "You're in love with her, aren't you? She's in love with you, isn't she? What more could you bring her?" Suddenly restless, she got up. "Get back on the saw and for me back to that hell-hot kitchen."

He didn't move for a time, watching Sharon until she disappeared into the house. Maybe she was a "bad woman," as his mother would have said, but he liked her. She'd had a hard life, he thought, and certainly one filled with disappointments, but still she had a quality of kindliness he had found in few people since he had thrown in with Bronco.

Well, he'd have it out with Bronco. Tonight. He wouldn't wait until Bronco came back from Winnemucca. He couldn't stay here that long. He'd go to Ruth. Still, if he could get even a little money out of Bronco . . .

He got up and began sawing again, condemning himself because he was still a boy dreaming a boy's dream. He'd get nothing from Bronco. He'd ask, but he'd get nothing. He might as well face the truth.

That evening Bronco came in late for supper. He was in a sour mood, barking at Sharon and morosely silent with Mark. As soon as they finished eating, Mark said: "I'm leaving, Bronco. I'm asking again for my wages."

"Damn it, you're not leaving," Bronco said harshly. "We're still partners. I don't know why I have to keep saying it. When Cross Seven shows a profit, you'll get your share. You've just got to make up your mind to wait."

He sat back with his usual rumbling belch, lit a cigar, and turned to Sharon. "You know that old goat of a Jacob Smith pretty well, don't you?"

"I know him, all right." She pushed her plate back. "What do you want to know about him?"

"We can use another herd," Bronco said. "I aim to make him send another one north. Next summer, I mean, after we've brought his cows through the winter and had a good calf crop, but Flagler says he won't do it."

"Flagler knows what he's talking about," Sharon said. "He was foreman of Smith's ranch on Quinn River for years. What do you think Smith sent him up here for?"

"To keep an eye on me," Bronco said sullenly.

"No. Smith wants him to get the lay of the land so he'll be able to ramrod Cross Seven when the time comes. When it does, Jacob will send his herd north, but you won't be around. When they're ready, they'll push over the hills into Sherman Valley and south against Nolan and Ardell. You're trying to use him, but what you don't know is that he figures on using you and has been from the first. Ever since he started buying Orry Andrews's steers, he's wanted a toehold up here, so, when you made your offer, you played right into his hand."

Bronco chewed on his cigar, muscles at the hinges of his jaws bunching into hard knots. He glared at Sharon, not believing a word she said.

"You've gone a long ways up, Bronco," Sharon said, "so you've got a long ways to go down. You won't stay up very long, either. The biggest mistake you ever made was to throw in with Jacob Smith. He doesn't have any children. Andy Wheeling is his heir, so he figures on Andy being the big poobah up here with Gene Flagler's help."

"That wet-nosed kid?" Bronco said incredulously. "Now I know you're crazy."

"That's a weakness of yours, not believing your friends," Sharon said. "When Jacob gets set, I mean when you're out of the way, they'll push south from here and north from Nevada, and they'll have Runyan, Nolan, and Ardell in a squeeze. In time they'll own the whole country and Jacob will have his second million." She leaned forward. "I tell you, I know him, Bronco. I've heard the silver dollars go chunk-chunk in his veins. His heart's a dollar sign. That's all it is."

Bronco rose and kicked back his chair. "You're full of horse manure. Maybe he's tough, but he's going to find out I'm tougher."

He stalked out of the room. Sharon smiled at Mark. "There goes a worried man, honey. You're the only friend he's got on this spread, and he's throwing you overboard."

There was no use talking to Bronco tonight, Mark knew. It was no better in the morning, Bronco burdened by worries as he was. Mark remembered what Herb Jackson and Matt Ardell had said, that he was going too far too fast.

He left at sunup with the steers, Gene Flagler going with him the first day, his face unsmiling. He said nothing to Mark when he left, and Mark wasn't sure Bronco had even seen him. The rest of the crew rode out, only Andy Wheeling remaining behind.

"I've been waiting for Curtis to get out of the way," Wheeling said. "You whipped me once, but you'll never do it again."

Mark stared at the lanky youth in surprise, not dreaming that Bronco had been responsible for Wheeling letting him alone. Now, looking at Wheeling, he saw the passionate hatred in the man's face, and he wasn't sure whether this was to be with fists or guns. All he could think of was that his revolver was in the house.

Then Wheeling drove at him, and Mark was relieved. He turned aside, slamming Wheeling on the side of the head and sending him reeling. Mark was no fighter and he knew it, but Wheeling was even less. The difference was that Wheeling fancied himself a fighting man, and that gave Mark an advantage.

Wheeling whirled and charged back, swinging from his boot tops. He was awkward and slow. Mark ducked under the punch and Wheeling was wide open. Mark caught him on the jaw, a sledge-hammer blow that snapped back his head, then Mark followed with another right while Wheeling was still reeling. The second punch knocked Wheeling down and piled him up against the corral, the back of his head hitting a post with an echoing thud.

For a moment Wheeling lay motionlessly, his eyes glassy, then he shook his head, rolled over, and reached for his gun. He had it clear of leather when Mark brought a boot hard against the man's wrist. Holding it there, he bent down, twisted the gun from Wheeling's hand, and stepped back.

"You had another try," Mark said, "and you came out the same way. Better forget it."

Wheeling swiped at the blood that ran down his chin from a cut lip. "Forget it, hell," he said hoarsely. "Next time it'll be with a gun."

Mark walked away, a strange queasiness working into his middle. Wheeling was the kind of madman who would do exactly what he'd threatened, and Mark wasn't sure he'd come out as well with a gun as he had with his fists.

When he went into the house for dinner, Sharon said: "I saw you handle Andy. I enjoyed it. Andy's a no-good brat who's been spoiled since the day he was born. Now he thinks he's one size bigger'n God because he's Jacob's nephew."

"I was lucky," Mark said.

"More than luck, I'd say," Sharon disagreed, "but I'll tell you one thing. Watch him, or he'll get you in the back."

At supper that night Sharon was strangely silent, her eyes on Mark, a bright expectancy in them. When he went to bed, he thought about putting a chair under the doorknob. There wasn't any lock. But he didn't. He took off his boots, shirt, and pants, and lay down on the bed, certain she would come, but not knowing for sure what he would do.

A few minutes later she did come, this time wearing only the lace robe. She closed the door and sat down on the bed. "You were expecting me, weren't you?" she asked.

When he didn't answer, she leaned over and tousled his hair. "I never saw hair as wiry as yours, honey," she said. "It kind of fits you. Bronco told me how he met you, your folks murdered and you blubbering 'cause you'd lost them, but he said you got tougher'n a boot heel before the summer was over. He ain't real proud of himself the way he performed when them Paiutes showed up, but he said you rubbed out three of 'em slicker'n goose grease."

She put her feet on the bed and sat on them, her thighs making a round bulge under the robe. "Funny thing about people. I figure you were raised by a couple of doting parents, so it wasn't what they did that put the iron in your backbone. It had to be there all the time, or Bronco wouldn't have brought it out." She shook her head. "Had to be something that was born in you, I guess, just like I was born to go to hell on a toboggan."

He didn't move. He felt hot and then cold as he lay there looking at her, knowing that all he needed to do was to reach for her, but he was thinking of what Bronco had said, about her giving him a dose, and then he'd give it to Ruth.

He said wearily: "Go away and leave me alone."

He saw the hurt that was in her face, then it left her and her face smoothed out. She said: "You want a piece just like any man. You've been fighting it ever since you came back. Bronco knew where I was coming tonight, damn his soul, and, when he gets back, he'll bat me around some."

She got up and pulled the robe more tightly around her. "It's good to be in love. I'd almost forgotten. It's sweet and full of dreams and promises. Don't lose it, Mark. Don't ever lose it."

She walked to the door as he got up and started putting on his shirt. "You're leaving now?"

He nodded. "Even after all the work I did, there's nothing for me here. Took me a long time to see it, but I finally did."

She smiled, as if thinking there was a better reason for his leaving. "It's best this way. I'll find a sack for your clothes."

He was dressed when she returned, his gun belt buckled around him. She waited while he stuffed everything he owned into the sack. He put on his sheepskin and picked up his rifle.

"Don't hate me, Mark," she said. "That's my trouble. I hate two men, Jacob Smith and Bronco Curtis, and I'll go on hating them as long as I live. I'm sorry for myself, but I can't help it."

"I'll never hate you, Sharon," he said.

He picked up the sack with his free hand. Then she came to him and put her arms around his neck, pulled his head down, and kissed him. "Good luck, honey. I wish I could come to your wedding, but it wouldn't do. I like you too much."

She picked up the lamp and held it for him at the head of the stairs. She was still standing there when he went out through the front door.

Chapter Seventeen

Going to the Circle J the next morning was the hardest thing Mark had ever done in his life. It wasn't just that Ruth and her father had been proved right about Bronco, and it wasn't just that Mark was coming back with his tail dragging. More than anything else, he was bothered by the fact that he didn't have a single cent in his pocket.

He had counted on getting a little money from Bronco, on being able to come to Ruth and say: "I've got enough money to buy you a ring and pay the preacher." Now all he could say was: "I love you and someday I'll be back." And yet he knew that if he said that, he might just as well keep on riding and never come back. Ruth had had enough waiting, maybe too much.

Mark left his sorrel in front of the house, the reins dragging. He saw Herb coming from the barn with a filled milk bucket, so he waited. Herb peered at him through his spectacles, as if trying to read his mind. He put the bucket down as he said: "Good morning, Mark. Have you come home to stay?"

Home! He should have known. Of course this was home, if home was where the people you loved lived. It wasn't Cross Seven. He should never have left here, but, if he hadn't, he wouldn't have known.

"I'd like to stay, Herb," he said.

Herb Jackson was not a man who found it easy to smile. He had almost forgotten how since he had discovered the bones of the horse he believed had belonged to Orry Andrews. But he smiled now, and laid a hand on Mark's shoulder as he said: "I'm glad, Mark. Ruth hasn't been worth shooting since you left. Come on in." Jackson pushed the spectacles back up on his nose and reached for the milk bucket.

They walked together to the back porch. Jackson opened the door and motioned for Mark to go in. Ruth was standing at the stove, frying flapjacks, her back to him. He said: "Ruth."

She whirled and cried out—"Mark!"—and ran to him. She put her arms around him and kissed him, and then clung to him, crying a little as she said: "Mark, don't ever go away again."

He knew then he had come back in time; he knew everything was all right and the money that he had thought was important wasn't important at all.

Jackson had taken the milk bucket into the pantry. Now he stood by the stove and blew his nose. When he could speak, he said gruffly: "Go wash up, Mark. I'm hungry."

Reluctantly Ruth let him go. She turned back to the stove, saying: "I'll bet you smelled breakfast. You got here just in time."

Mark washed, then tried to comb his wiry hair and gave up in disgust. He returned to the kitchen and sat down. Ruth poured the coffee and returned to the table, and Jackson said grace. When he finished, Mark said: "I might just as well get it said. You were right about Bronco. I was working for nothing, so I've got nothing. I'm mighty sore about it, too. I guess I've got a right to be."

Jackson helped himself to the flapjacks and passed the platter to Mark, then reached for the pitcher of syrup. "You had to find out for yourself, Mark. Nobody could tell you, which is natural enough."

Ruth had recovered from the shock of having Mark back. She said sharply: "I could have told him."

Jackson lifted his head and looked at her. "Ruth, you keep honing your tongue to a fine edge and you'll be able to peel potatoes with it pretty soon."

Her face turned red. "I'm sorry, Mark."

"I know how you feel, if Ruth doesn't," Jackson said. "Curtis was with you the day your folks were buried, and he gave you the schooling you had to have to make out by yourself. He's a hard man, and a little of that hardness rubbed off on you. Not much. Just enough. It's natural that you'd be grateful, and that you'd keep hoping to find some goodness in him that isn't there. He's bad, Mark, as completely bad as any man I ever met."

Mark thought about the first summer they had ridden together, of Bronco's buying food and clothes for him, and cartridges after his money was gone so he could learn to handle a gun. He thought about their winter together on Cross Seven and about Bronco's dreams, which included Mark. If he had never made the connection with Jacob Smith, Mark was convinced that Bronco would have kept on including him, that at the time Bronco meant what he said.

But there was no use arguing with Jackson, so he only asked: "Is any man all bad, Herb?"

"I deserved that," Jackson admitted. "There's some of God in all of us and some of the devil, and we're all on kind of a teeter board. It's just that with Curtis the devil outweighs God."

They didn't talk any more until they finished eating, then Jackson leaned back and filled his pipe. Mark knew he didn't dare say anything about going away again and coming back with money in his pocket. They wanted him and maybe they even needed him, and so he would have to stay. He wanted to. Maybe that was the important thing.

He glanced at Ruth, who was watching him intently and waiting for him to speak, but he didn't know what to say. Maybe he could live here and work through the winter, and by spring he would have a little money, if Jackson could afford to pay him anything.

But Jackson stopped that kind of thinking when he said: "You kids have been pulling and hauling at each other about getting married. I don't see any sense in putting it off. There's a preacher in Scott City. Go see him, Mark. Fact is, I've got a little jag of steers to take to the fort today. You can help me drive them, and then go on over to Scott City. It's not far."

"Maybe you'd better let Mark speak for himself," Ruth said in the same sharp tone she'd used before. "I'm not sure he even wants to marry me."

He looked at her across the table, the early morning sun touching her dark hair and bringing it alive. For the first time he thought he understood. She had made advances and he had not responded as she hoped he would. She had her pride about that just as he had his pride about money, pride that had become a wedge and had driven them apart, and suddenly he realized this was the most important moment of his life. He must lift the wedge and throw it away; he would never have another chance as good as this.

Mark was aware of the silence that had fallen upon them, broken only by the snapping of the pine wood in the stove and the hammering of the clock on a shelf by the window.

"Ruth," he said, "I love you so much it hurts sometimes. I would be honored if you would be my wife, but I have nothing to offer you except my love. Is that enough?"

She opened her mouth and closed it and swallowed, and finally said in a small voice: "It's all I ever wanted, Mark."

Jackson rose, his pipe clutched between his teeth. He said around the pipe stem: "I'll catch that bay for you, Mark. You'll need a fresh horse."

He left the kitchen, and Mark came around the table and Ruth rose and ran into his arms. After he had kissed her, she said: "It's funny, Mark. I would have married you a year ago when you came for Sunday dinner. Remember?"

"I'll never forget it," he said, and knew it was better this way. He hadn't been ready then, but he was now. It wasn't the months and years that counted, but the heat of events in the crucible of life that fused and changed a boy into a man. He was surprised at the way the thought came to him. He must have heard Jackson say it sometime. He smiled at her as he asked: "Can you give me the date so I can tell the preacher?"

She considered a moment, then said: "Would this Friday be too soon? Today's Monday. That would give us most of a week to get ready."

"Tomorrow wouldn't be too soon," he said, and kissed her again. "Guess I better go help Herb."

They delivered the herd to the fort shortly after noon, and Jackson was paid $312. As they rode away, Jackson divided the money and gave Mark half of it. "No argument, son. Our partnership will be a real one, not the kind Curtis talked about."

"But I haven't done anything to earn it," Mark said.

"You have, and you will." From habit Jackson reached up and pushed his spectacles back on the bridge of his nose. "Mark, I like you and I welcome you as a son-in-law, and with your help we can run twice as many cattle as I have under the Circle J iron. But there's more to this than that. I'm relieved because I know you'll look out for Ruth. I'm not fooling myself. I'm a walking dead man, and I have been ever since Gene Flagler took that shot at me."

"Not if you stay off Cross Seven range."

"That's something I can't do. Don't ask me to explain it. You won't understand it any more than Ruth could understand why you had to go back to the Cross Seven."

Jackson took a long breath. "There's another thing. Did Flagler mean what he said about Cross Seven coming across the hills next year?"

Mark nodded. "Providing Bronco can get Jacob Smith to send another herd north."

Jackson shook his head, frowning. "I'll never sell, so you see I need you more than ever. I couldn't fight them off alone. Maybe we can together." They had reached the junction with the Agency road, and Jackson motioned toward a cluster of buildings to the west. "Go see the preacher, Mark. I'll tell Ruth you'll be late."

Let Herb have his dreams, Mark thought as he rode toward Scott City. They'd have no chance either alone or together against the Cross Seven crew if Bronco made the move he had threatened, but that danger was eight or nine months away. He refused to worry about it now.

He was surprised when he reached Scott City that so much town could have sprouted out of the sagebrush since the Indian trouble. Not that it was much of a town, but last June there had been nothing.

He rode slowly, noting the store with Robert Cameron's name on the false front, the saloon, the hotel, the livery stable, and the blacksmith shop, the buildings strung out on both sides of the road without any visible plan. He saw ten or twelve houses at both ends of the town, and he was fifty yards beyond the store before he saw the church, a squat, homely building with a cross in front.

A cottage as graceless as the church stood a few yards to the west; a sign in front read Rev. Sylvester Jones. Mark stepped down and knocked on the door. The man who opened the door was tall and ungainly with an Adam's apple that bobbed uncertainly as he said: "Good afternoon." Mark noticed that the preacher's hair needed trimming and was reminded of his own.

"You the preacher?"

"I'm Reverend Sylvester Jones."

"I'm getting married Friday night at the Circle J. Will you perform the ceremony?"

"I shall be honored," Jones said. "At what hour?"

Mark hesitated. Ruth hadn't told him. He said: "Eight o'clock."

"I shall be there." Jones extended his hand. "Congratulations. Your name, sir?"

"Mark Kelton."

"I'm pleased to meet you." The Adam's apple bobbed as the preacher swallowed. "Mister Kelton, I would be remiss in my duty as a man of God if I did not inquire as to the salvation of your soul and that of your bride. I consider it a matter of primary importance that a young couple be united with their Savior when a family is being started."

"I can't say about my soul," Mark said, "but I guess God would be mighty happy to save the soul of my bride. Her name is Ruth Jackson, if you need it. Good day, sir."

He strode back to his horse, resolved to break the reverend's neck if he tried to turn the wedding into an evangelistic meeting. He stopped at the store and bought a wedding ring from Robert Cameron, a dour, long-necked Scotsman who had founded the town, then examined the suits and bought one for $18 dollars that fit reasonably well, and a white shirt and tie.

As he left the store, the suit, which had been wrapped in butcher paper, under his arm, he saw Matt Ardell come out of the saloon across the street. Ardell stopped, not recognizing him for a moment, then, when he did, he called: "Mark, I want to see you!" Ardell stepped down off the saloon porch and strode through the ankle-deep dust. "Damned if I knew you for a minute. The last time I saw you, you were in bed. You've changed some since then."

He held out his hand, and Mark took it. "I feel better than I did the last time you saw me."

"You've grown," Ardell said. "You're as tall as Bronco. Come on over and have a drink. I was starting home, but a few minutes either way won't make no difference."

Mark didn't want to linger in town, for it would be dark now before he got back to the Circle J, but he couldn't afford to turn Ardell down. The rancher was as fat as ever, his voice as squeaky as ever, and he had an infectious friendliness about him that reminded Mark how much he had liked the man when they'd met at the fort.

"Glad to," Mark said, and followed Ardell into the saloon.

Both ordered beer and sat down at a rough pine table near a front window. When the bartender retreated to the other side of the room, Ardell leaned forward and said in a low tone: "I'm glad I ran into you. Been hearing some talk I don't like. Remember I told you to slow Bronco down?"

"Nobody can slow him down," Mark said. "Least of all me. I've left the Cross Seven, and I'm living at the Circle J. I'm marrying Ruth Jackson Friday night. I hope you can come to the wedding."

"By golly, I will," Ardell said, and shook hands with Mark. "Congratulations. She's too good for you, son."

"I know," Mark said, "but don't tell her."

Ardell laughed. "I won't. Never let a woman know she's too good for a man. Most of 'em think it anyway. Now what about you 'n' Bronco? I thought you were partners?"

"He wanted cheap help," Mark said, and drank his beer.

He wondered how much he should tell Ardell. If it had been either John Runyan or Dave Nolan, he wouldn't have said anything, but there was a simple honesty about Ardell that made him trust the man.

So he told Ardell what had happened as briefly as he could, leaving out only the part that Sharon Sanders had played. When he finished, Ardell said: "I ain't surprised. By God, I ain't. That's why I said what I did about slowing him up. He's as crazy as a man eating locoweed. He could have stayed in Ten Mile Valley for fifty years and had a good spread and been friends with everybody, but the minute he threw in with Jacob Smith, I knew what would happen. So'd Dave Nolan. I dunno 'bout John Runyan. He don't cotton much to Bronco after he plugged Monk Evans, but he's scared of Jacob Smith."

Ardell finished his beer, then wiped the foam off his mouth with his sleeve. "Gene Flagler's a tough nut. Some of what you just said has come to me, a little here and a little there. That's why I wanted to gab with you a minute."

He scratched a droopy cheek. "I dunno, Mark. Damned if I do. If we've got to fight, we oughta do it before Jacob Smith sends an army of gunfighters up here, but then again maybe it'll blow over. Part of it depends on how Bronco makes out through the winter. Depends on Runyan, too. If we could get some iron into his backbone and he closed his range so Cross Seven cattle couldn't cross it, they wouldn't be getting to Winnemucca in such good shape and Bronco would be up a tree."

Ardell rose. "Well, I've got to ride. Be morning now before I get home. I'll see you Friday night. Me 'n' my missus. Maybe Dave Nolan and his wife, too. So long, Mark."

Mark followed him outside and waited until he heaved himself into the saddle and rode away, turning back once to lift a big hand in a farewell gesture. Mark crossed the street and mounted, wondering if Ardell and Nolan would really come to the wedding, and, if they did, what would Bronco think when he heard?

Bronco was sure they'd come to his housewarming because they were afraid of Jacob Smith, but Mark had a hunch that of the three cowmen, Bronco would see only John Runyan.

* * * * *

After Mark finished his late supper, he showed Ruth the ring. She tried it on and found that Mark had made a good guess as to size. She admired his suit, and then he had her trim his hair. After she had gone to bed, Mark told Jackson about his talk with Ardell.

Jackson sat on his chair, listening closely, shoulders hunched forward, face in his hands, and, when Mark finished, he said in a troubled voice: "It was a wonderful country, Mark, before the people came."

Chapter Eighteen

The days from Tuesday morning until Friday evening were frantic ones for Ruth and her father and intolerable ones for Mark, who didn't know what to do or what was expected of him. He did the chores and chopped wood until he had a pile as tall as the woodshed, and, when he got tired, he just sat on the chopping block and wondered what had happened to him.

Jackson rode to the fort on Tuesday morning and asked Mrs. Bolton to stay with Ruth and help her get ready. The rest of the time he was riding over Sherman Valley, inviting people to come to the wedding. If it had been left up to Mark, he would have had no one there but Ruth and the preacher, but he soon discovered he was the forgotten man, that nothing was required of him except to stay out of the way.

Jackson opened his ancient cowhide trunk and lifted out two silver candlesticks that Ruth and Mrs. Bolton polished until they could see their faces in them. Then he took out Ruth's mother's wedding dress, and for two days nothing went on in the house but cutting and fitting and pinning and sewing.

If Mark or Jackson wanted something to eat, one of them had to rustle it. Mrs. Bolton apparently had her mouth full of pins from sunup to sundown and was as nervous as a heifer with triplets. If Mark poked his head into the front room, she was as likely as not to throw a stove stick at him and mumble: "Scat."

It seemed to Mark that the situation would be simplified if Mrs. Bolton swallowed the pins and died of a perforated stomach. Mark had cause to recast his entire attitude toward the state of matrimony, and he found himself in complete sympathy with Lieutenant Bolton's dedication to the cause of Indian fighting.

To Mark the greatest enigma of all was Herb Jackson. He had liked Jackson from the first time he had met him more than a year ago, but he had never pretended to understand him. Jackson was a deep-thinking man who loved to listen to his own monologues and who hated injustice of any kind.

But he was also a lonely man. He had often told Mark that Orry Andrews had been his only close friend, but now he was bent on getting the biggest crowd that he could to the wedding. This made no sense to Mark, so he finally quit trying to understand it.

Mark wished that Bronco could stand up with him, but by this time Bronco was probably in Winnemucca. Even if he were home, Mark could not have asked him to come to Herb Jackson's house. Time after time through these four hectic days Mark wished he could talk to someone about the marriage relationship. There had been a day when he could have talked to Bronco, but Bronco wouldn't have known anything. Besides, he could not share Bronco's attitude toward women.

He could have talked to Sharon Sanders if she had been anywhere except on Cross Seven. Not that she knew anything about marriage, but at least she would have been sympathetic. His mind, more often than he wanted it to, conjured up the picture of her coming into his room that last night he was at Cross Seven, wearing nothing but the lace robe. He was titillated by it, yet he never regretted telling her to go away and leave him alone.

That left no one but Herb Jackson, and Mark could never quite bring himself to opening up the question with him. Only once did Jackson come close to mentioning it. That was on Thursday evening when Mark was milking, and Jackson, who had just ridden in, came to stand in the runway behind the cow Mark was milking.

"I guess you know my life is bound up in Ruth," Jackson said, speaking slowly as if he were choosing each word carefully. "I don't know of any other man I would give her to except you. You've heard me say her mother died when she was little. Well, I've raised her the best way I could, but there are times when I realize I've never really understood her. She's pretty headstrong at times. The only advice I can give you is to be patient with her."

Mark looked up at Jackson's face, and in the thin dusk light he saw the somber cast to it and sensed that even now Jackson had doubts about the wisdom of the marriage. Probably he would have opposed it at this time if he had not felt, as he had once said, that he was a walking dead man.

"I'll try, Herb," Mark said. "I guess the main thing both of us want is to make her happy."

"I'm sure it is," Jackson agreed. "I hope I live long enough to see my first grandchild."

That was a strange thing for a man as young as Jackson to say, but Mark understood why he said it. He would be drawn back to Cross Seven range time after time, and the odds were he'd go once too often.

Ruth and Mrs. Bolton worked in the kitchen all day Friday, baking cakes and pies and making sandwiches, then they disappeared upstairs. Mark, shaved and bathed, polished his boots, and, with Jackson's help, put on his new shirt and store suit. His fingers trembled, and there was a great yawning abyss where his stomach should have been.

Then the people began coming, on horses, in buggies and carts, even in spring wagons. Lieutenant Bolton and Captain Gatskill from the fort arrived in a surrey behind a team of matched bays. Shortly before eight Matt Ardell and Dave Nolan drove up with their wives. The Reverend Sylvester Jones had been on hand for an hour, working hard at shaking hands, his Adam's apple reacting with more than usual enthusiasm.

Just before eight o'clock Mrs. Bolton came downstairs to see that everyone and everything was in order. At this late season of the year there were no flowers, so Mrs. Bolton had prepared a vase of artificial roses, which she had set on the table in the center of the room, the silver candlesticks on both sides of the vase.

Now she lit the candles, saw to it that the preacher and Mark were exactly where they should be, and that Jackson was at the foot of the stairs. She had to plow through the crowd, shoving people here and there, but she achieved everything she set out to do in a remarkably short time. Then she disappeared, and a moment later Ruth started down the stairs, moving slowly and gracefully.

Mark, his eyes fixed on Ruth, knew, in this moment, that he had never seen any woman as beautiful as Ruth and never would in the future. Her wedding dress was a cream brocade turned a little yellow by age and trimmed with Spanish lace.

Her blue-black hair had been carefully and skillfully curled; her brown eyes seemed black at this distance. They searched for Mark and found him, and she smiled, her front teeth small and white and perfect. He tried to swallow the lump in his throat, and failed, and he wondered if he could say the simple words . . . "I do."

Ruth came on down the stairs and through the narrow aisle that the crowd gave her, a hand resting on her father's arm, and it seemed to Mark that he was standing off somewhere at the side, watching this scene, that the tall, slender youth with the unruly hair waiting by the table was someone else, someone he had known before. Briefly he thought of his parents, then that scene was blotted out, for it did not belong to this time or place. It had happened a long time ago, and life had changed for him since then.

It was over, and Mark must have said—"I do."—although afterward he could not remember having said it. He kissed Ruth, the moment one of infinite tenderness, and then the crowd moved in against them, and people were shaking his hand and slapping him on the back and saying: "The biggest wedding Sherman Valley ever seen, and the prettiest bride. By golly, she is." And Dave Nolan, small and precise and as strong as the fine metal that went into the main spring of a watch, shook hands, saying: "Congratulations, Mark." Outside, people were squeezed into the open door and against the windows, trying not to miss anything.

After that the furniture was moved out of the room or against the wall, and Pigeon-Toed Mike, from near the head of Doolin Creek, tuned up his fiddle and began to play. Mark danced once with Ruth, awkward and with feet ten yards long, it seemed, and, when she looked up at him, giving him her smile, he felt big and proud and stout enough to lick any five men in the world.

At midnight they stopped to eat, and Matt Ardell and Dave Nolan got Mark and Herb Jackson in the corner. "We've been talking," Ardell said. "About Curtis and Smith. If it comes to a showdown, you won't be alone. We figure the summit of Paradise Hills is the west boundary of Cross Seven, and we're aiming to see that it keeps on being the boundary."

"I'll hold my present boundaries," Nolan said. "I'm not worried about what Cross Seven can do to me, but it'll raise hell if Curtis starts shoving you little ranchers out of the way. We can't afford to stand for it, and we won't."

Jackson shook hands with both men and thanked them, acting surprised that the two big men of the valley would be interested in the welfare of the Circle J. More dancing after that, with Matt Ardell and his wife, who was as fat as he was, cavorting around like kids and having a wonderful time.

Mrs. Nolan, a frail, pretty woman, spent most of her time in a chair next to the wall, her husband standing beside her. Now that Mrs. Bolton had done her job, she surprised Mark by dancing with the lieutenant as if this were the last good time she would have on earth.

Mark, feeling as if he were a spectator while all the world whirled by, marveled at the way everyone had a good time, dancing with the gusto of people who had few such opportunities and were bent on making the most of this one.

Suddenly the party broke up in a fashion that surprised and shocked Mark, who had not expected it. Some of the women descended on Ruth and hustled her up the stairs. Then the men, Matt Ardell leading them, seized Mark and carried him up the stairs in spite of his resistance. They dumped him on the bed and left, laughing and calling back—"Good night!"—along with some remarks that embarrassed him.

Ruth was sitting on the side of the bed, her hair rumpled, looking as if she suddenly felt very much alone. He reached over and pulled her to him and kissed her, but she was stiff and restrained and could not fully surrender to him.

He got up and looked around. This was Ruth's room. He had never been in it before. It was very feminine with cheesecloth covering the walls and pictures pinned to the cloth. Her clothes hung from pegs driven into the logs. Her comb and brush and perfume bottles and a music box were on the dresser, and the scent of sachet powder permeated the air.

Outside, there was a great deal of racket, people calling to each other and hooking up their rigs and then driving away. Then there was silence, and Ruth still sat on the other side of the bed staring at Mark as if in these moments he had become a stranger.

He sat down beside her, not knowing what to say or do, but knowing he must say something. He took her hands, asking: "Tired?"

"A little."

"You were beautiful tonight when you came down the stairs," he said. "The most beautiful woman I ever saw."

"Oh, Mark," she whispered, and threw her arms around him. "I love you more than anything in the world."

They sat there for a time on the edge of the bed, his arm around her, her head on his shoulder. Dawn was beginning to explore the room when she turned her face to his and kissed him, and said, her mouth close to his ear: "Mark, let's go to bed."

Chapter Nineteen

December was a dry month, the sun shining every day from a cloudless sky, but giving little warmth to a cold, dusty earth. At night the stars were sparkling lamps hung in a clear sky, so big and brilliant, Herb Jackson said, that it seemed a man could reach out and touch them. Then he shook his head and said he wished it would snow. They'd all feel better if it did. Besides, this was a fool's paradise. Too much good weather now meant extra bad weather later on.

But Mark refused to worry about extra bad weather that was coming. To him these weeks were perfect, so why question them? Or mar perfection by dreaming up troubles that might happen later? The old life was behind him, and he was content to let it stay behind him.

Now that time had given him perspective, he understood Bronco Curtis. Or thought he did. As long as Bronco had needed him, they had been partners, and Bronco had probably meant all the things he had said, but once Bronco had hooked up with Jacob Smith, he had no more need for Mark. So the partnership was dissolved, perhaps without Bronco's actually realizing how it had happened, or why.

In any case, Mark had no regrets over what had happened. Bronco had taught him what he had to know, and for that Mark would always be grateful. The worry about coming to Ruth empty-handed no longer burdened him. She was happy. All he had to do was to look at her and know that. Besides, Herb Jackson needed him. That was easy to see, too.

Being broke was not important, Mark knew. In this country the rich could be counted on the fingers of one hand; with everyone else, being broke was the common condition. What a man was and what he could do were the important things. Once Mark understood that, the bitterness he had felt toward Bronco was gone.

On the Sunday before Christmas Ruth told Mark it was time to get a tree, so he saddled their horses and they rode into the timber, searching until they found a small pine shaped exactly the way Ruth wanted it. As they rode back to the house, the sun dropping toward the western rim, the thought occurred to Mark that life was not meant to be perfect, that it was like the weather. If it was too good now, it was bound to be extra bad later on.

He made a stand by lantern light, and they spent the evening decorating the tree. The tinsel was tarnished by age, and Ruth could find only three shiny balls. "Most of them got broken when we moved here," she said, "and we haven't been able to buy any since then. Maybe Cameron has some in the store."

"I'm going to town tomorrow," Mark said. "I'll see."

"Get some candles, too, if he has any." Ruth held one up that was about an inch long, and grimaced. "We haven't been able to buy any that would fit the holders. Every Christmas we light these for just a little while and then blow them out, but we can't nurse them along much more."

"I'll look for some," Mark promised.

Herb had made a shiny star out of a tin can. Mark tied it to the top of the tree, then he and Ruth popped corn and strung it, Herb sitting in his rocking chair and watching. He refused to help decorate.

"That's for the young," he said. "One of the great tragedies of life is the fact that, as you get older, it's hard to catch the

Christmas spirit." He laughed softly. "But it's contagious. By Christmas Eve I'll have it."

"You'd better," Ruth said threateningly. "We're not going to have any old Scrooge around here who can't say Merry Christmas."

"That's right," Mark agreed. "When I was home, I thought we had some pretty trees, but this is the prettiest one I ever saw. Maybe it's like the moon, reflected beauty, if you have a pretty girl in the house."

Ruth giggled. "You're a liar," she said, "but your lies are nice to hear."

The next day he rode into town, the first time he had been in Scott City since he'd bought Ruth's ring and his wedding suit. A new building had gone up beside the store, the tall letters across the false front reading SHARON'S CAFÉ.

Mark tied in front of Cameron's store, wondering about Sharon's identity. It was not a common name, but he didn't think it would be Sharon Sanders. As far as he knew, she was still living with Bronco on the Cross Seven. Besides, he didn't think she was the kind who would try to make a living by running a restaurant.

He went into the store. He greeted Cameron, then said: "I've got to buy some Christmas presents, but I sure don't know what they'll be."

"Look around," Cameron said. "You might get some ideas. I've got a few books yonder on that shelf. Your father-in-law is a reading man. He might like one."

Mark knew that Jackson liked Dickens, so he bought *A Tale of Two Cities*. He had trouble finding anything for Ruth, but he finally decided on some white-and-pink checked cloth he thought would make a dress she would like, and added some small items he knew she needed—a spool of white thread, a thimble, and a package of needles.

As Cameron wrapped his purchases, Mark asked: "Who's the Sharon that runs the restaurant?"

Cameron glanced at him quickly and lowered his gaze to the cord he was tying around Mark's package. "Sharon Sanders. She told me to ask you to see her the first time you were in town, but I sure would have forgotten if you hadn't reminded me."

Mark hesitated, not wanting to see the woman, yet feeling that he should. Finally he said: "I'll stop in for a minute."

"You'd better," Cameron said, "or she'll have a piece of my hide. She wants to give you a meal for old times' sake, she told me."

Mark paid the storekeeper, went outside, and tied his package behind the saddle. For a time he stood staring at the front of the restaurant, wondering where Sharon had got the money to start a business. She had claimed she was broke when Bronco brought her to Cross Seven, and Mark doubted that Bronco would have given her the money if he had it.

He walked past the hitch pole and went in, the smell of baking bread coming to him. Sharon heard the door close and came out of the kitchen. "Mark!" she cried. "Mark, I'm glad to see you. I thought you never were coming to town."

She ran to him and kissed him, then drew back, embarrassed. "I forgot you were a married man now. If anybody saw that, your wife would hear and you'd be in a peck of trouble. I'd be in it, too, if Mister Cameron saw me kissing you. I'm going to marry him, you know."

She laughed, seeing the expression of shocked surprise on his face. "Sure, it isn't like me to get married. You know it, and that god-damned Bronco Curtis knows it. So does Jacob Smith. But Mister Cameron don't, so I'd take it kindly if you didn't tell him."

"I won't," Mark said.

"Oh, hell, I knew you wouldn't, but I ain't so sure Bronco won't when he hears. He allowed he was going to run me out of the country, and I allowed he wasn't. I talked Mister Cameron into putting up this building for me and loaning me the money to get started. He takes his meals here, and a few people drop in for supper. Trouble is there ain't many folks who come to town during the winter, but I'll do better, come summer." She took his arm. "Let's go on back to the kitchen. This ain't a fitting place for friends to talk."

"I can't stay," Mark said. "Cameron told me you wanted to see me when I came to town, so I just dropped in to say howdy. I've . . ."

"You're not in that big a hurry. Been a long time since breakfast. I'll fix you something."

"Too early for dinner," he said. "Just a cup of coffee."

"All right, if that's what you want." She led him past the counter and row of stools into the kitchen and pulled up a rocking chair for him. "You sit down there now and let me look at you." She put her hands on her hips, smiling at him. "Mark, you look happy. You never did when you were on the Cross Seven, but that's something I can understand. Nobody's happy there. I'm glad you pulled out and got married. You've got a good life, ain't you?"

"Yes, a good life," he said.

She poured a cup of coffee and gave it to him, then sat down in front of him. "Mark, I've been wanting to talk to you. I was gonna get a buggy and drive out to see you, but I kept thinking you'd come to town. I guess I was kind of afraid, too. They say a good woman can always tell a bad woman, so I thought I'd wait until I married Mister Cameron. I'd be a good woman then, you see. That's all it takes."

He stirred his coffee, looking at her and sensing a bitterness that he had not felt in her when she was on Cross Seven. She'd never had any illusions about herself, but she'd been able to accept the kind of life she led. Now she was reaching for respectability, and he had a notion she was regretting what she had been to Jacob Smith and Bronco Curtis.

"How'd you happen to leave Cross Seven?" he asked.

"Leave it?" She shouted the words, glaring at him. "By God, don't you know?" She shook her head. "No, of course you wouldn't. Well, I'll tell you. Bronco fired me. That's why I left. When he got back from Winnemucca, he kicked my tail off the ranch the minute he found out you'd gone. Blamed me for you leaving, he did. I tried to tell him it was his own fault, working you to death and not giving you anything. I reminded him that you told him you were leaving, but it just made him mad."

She was red in the face, so angry she was trembling. "I never hated nobody in my life before I met Bronco, not even Jacob Smith, who is a greedy old booger, but I hate Bronco. I guess I thought I was in love with him." She pointed a finger at herself. "Can you imagine that, me thinking I was in love with any man? I don't love Mister Cameron, but I'll show him a good time, and I'll see to it he won't ever be sorry he married me."

She took Mark's cup and filled it again and gave it back to him. "Hell, I ought to have known about Bronco. If anybody ought to know a man, I should. Trouble is, Bronco's the kind you can't help liking, even when you know he's a bastard."

She leaned forward and tapped Mark on the knee. "You know something, Mark? Bronco won't last another year. All his big plans and dreams won't amount to a damn. He was gonna have a big housewarming, you know, and make the nabobs come to Cross Seven. He didn't. Oh, he tried, but they didn't come. He got the idea that when you got up in the world, you could make folks do things. He found out he was wrong. Now he'll find out why Jacob Smith threw in with him. Jacob will clean him out right down to his last dime, and I'll laugh in his face if I get the chance. If a man ever deserved what he gets, it'll be Bronco Curtis."

Mark finished his coffee, remembering the summer he had ridden with Bronco and how Bronco had, as he put it, "nursed a wet-nose kid." Well, he had more than paid Bronco back, working for him as long as he had and getting nothing for it.

He rose. "I've got to mosey, Sharon. Thanks for the coffee."

She took his cup and set it on the table. Then she said as if she couldn't understand it: "You were his one friend and he treated you like dirt, but you don't hate him, do you?"

"No," Mark said. "I don't hate him. Not any more."

"You will," she said. "Before you're done, you'll hate him enough to kill him. You'll see."

Mark thought of Herb Jackson, who was obsessed with the conviction that Bronco had killed Orry Andrews and therefore must be punished. If Bronco killed Jackson, Mark would hate him enough to kill him. Or if, as Flagler had threatened, they came over the ridge next summer and drove Jackson and Ruth and Mark off the Circle J, he would hate him for that enough to kill him. Maybe he would.

But not now. "I don't hate anybody, Sharon," he said. "I'm happy. If you're going to marry Cameron, you ought to be, too."

She scowled, not liking the advice, then she laughed. "You sound just like the preacher. Well, thanks for the sermon."

"You're welcome," he said, "and thanks for the coffee."

He went out, looking back once when he reached the door and lifting a hand to her. She waved to him, calling: "Come back and I'll give you a free meal!"

He thought about her as he rode home, and then about Bronco, and he was a little surprised that he didn't hate Bronco. Broken promises. Smashed dreams. Empty pockets. But, no, they weren't enough. Not to make him hate Bronco. He owed Bronco too much. Besides, this was Christmas.

That night after he and Ruth had gone to bed, she told him she was pregnant. She slipped a hand under his head and pulled him to her and held him hard, whispering: "It's what I want. I don't have much of a Christmas present for you. That's why I wanted to tell you. I hoped you'd think it was the best present I could give you."

For just a moment he was stunned. This was something he had not thought about very much. They hadn't even talked about it. His first thought was for her, and he said: "You can't have a baby. There's no doctor here."

She laughed. "I'm afraid I can. Honey, don't worry about me. Women have babies without doctors all the time. Missus Bolton will come out and stay with me. She's helped several of the women at the fort. I'll be all right."

He took a long breath. "It's something I've got to get used to. But I like the idea, if you're sure you'll be all right." He hesitated, then added: "You're sure you will be all right?"

"Of course, silly." She kissed him, and added softly: "I'm glad you're glad, Mark."

He drew back so that he was free of her arm, and then drew her to him. "You sleep on my arm," he said, "and I'll lie here and think about it. If it's a girl, can I name it?"

"It?" she scoffed. "It'll be a her, not an it."

"Well, can I?"

"Of course you can," she said drowsily.

She went to sleep, his arm around her as was their habit, her head on his shoulder, and he thought about the time Herb had said that neither he nor Ruth had made the crossing to manhood and womanhood. They had now, he knew. This would, indeed, be a Merry Christmas.

Chapter Twenty

Herb Jackson's prophecy that too much good weather in the early part of the winter meant extra bad weather later on turned out exactly right. Snow began falling on the last day in January and kept on intermittently until it was three feet deep on the valley floor and deeper in the hill country to the north.

In February the weather turned warm, then bitterly cold, and the snow crusted with ice. From then on until the thaw came Mark and Herb Jackson fought a daily battle to keep the small Circle J herd alive.

For weeks there was no communication between the Circle J and Scott City, or with the neighboring ranches. For a time the snow was too deep. Then, after it went off, every ravine and creekbed was filled with rushing torrents that pounded down from the mountains north of the Circle J and spread out over the valley so that for a time it had the appearance of an enormous lake. The earth, waterlogged, could absorb no more.

Even after the water had receded, the valley floor was a great bog for weeks, making travel so difficult that no one left his ranch except for an emergency, and it was sheer emergency that brought men to the Circle J, begging for hay.

"They're crazy," Herb told Mark. "They ought to know we don't have any to spare. Besides, how would they haul it? All the roads in the valley would mire a snipe."

But crazy or not, they kept coming, all of them telling incredible stories of their winter loss. They had been almost wiped out, and they would be if they didn't get hay. The tales they carried about Dave Nolan and Matt Ardell were even worse. Neither Rocking Chair nor Bearpaw had brought enough cattle through the winter to furnish beef for the crews next summer.

No one seemed to know anything about Bronco Curtis and the Cross Seven or John Runyan and his Triangle R, and no one cared. At a time like this men thought only of themselves and their own futures. When Herb told them he couldn't spare a forkful of hay and that he'd be lucky to pull his own cattle through the spring until the grass was up, they cursed him and said, if it was the other way around, they'd divide the hay they had.

"It's a sad side of human nature that comes out under these conditions," Herb told Mark and Ruth one evening at supper. "I've always put up more hay than anyone else in the country. I've carried a good deal over from one year to the next, and more than one man has laughed at me for it. Now I'm a miser and a son-of-a-bitch because I won't share what we've got."

"They want you to share their misery," Ruth said.

"Or bring you down to their level," Mark added. "If half the yarns they tell are true, you're the richest man in the valley."

"We are the richest men, you mean," Herb corrected him, and sighed. "It can't be as bad as they say. Some of them claim you can walk from Nolan's house clean across the valley to Ardell's by stepping on carcasses and not put your foot on the ground."

"That must be true," Ruth said, "judging from the smell when the wind's right."

Mark nodded, knowing the stench would get worse when the warm weather came. He couldn't keep from wondering how Bronco had fared, but he didn't mention it to Herb or Ruth, and Bronco was one man who had not showed up, begging for hay.

"It must be hell," Mark said, "to be in Nolan's and Ardell's shoes."

"The higher you go," Jackson observed, "the farther you've got to fall."

That was true, Mark thought, an observation that was typical of Herb Jackson, who wanted only enough wealth to provide him with a living. There would be great opportunities here before the summer was over, buying neighboring ranches for practically nothing, the kind of opportunities that would drive Bronco crazy trying to take advantage of them if he were in Herb's place. But that kind of greed wasn't in Herb Jackson. He contended that in the long run a man was better off to depend only on himself, to stay out of debt and be clear of bankers and storekeepers like Robert Cameron in Scott City.

Mark talked about it at night when he and Ruth were in bed and didn't have to worry about Herb hearing them. "It's not just us," Mark said. "I mean you and me. We've got our children to think of. This is the chance of a lifetime. If we don't grab, someone else will. Bronco, if he's still in business. Or Jacob Smith."

"What can Dad do?" Ruth asked. "You know he doesn't have much money."

"Borrow," Mark said. "He can get money in Cañon City. By fall we could have the whole north end of the valley. We won't have another winter like this for fifty years. In a little while we'd be as big as Rocking Chair or Bearpaw was last summer."

Ruth sighed. "It would be nice to be rich, but you know how Dad is. He's never been in debt in his life. He won't start now."

"I'm supposed to be his partner," Mark said doggedly.

"But he's the senior partner, and he has the last word," Ruth said. "In anything like this, he'll do what he believes in. I think in anything else, he'd let you do what you wanted to. The truth is, he doesn't want to be rich. He says it's bad for a person."

So Mark said nothing to Herb, for he knew it would only lead to an argument. In his own way, Herb Jackson was just as stubborn as Bronco Curtis. The right attitude was somewhere between, Mark thought, but he had made his choice when he came here. He had known how Herb felt; he had known that Herb would never change.

In time he would have to break with Herb just as he had broken with Bronco. He would have to be his own man; he had to have the right to make his own decisions, but for the time being he was helpless, and he made up his mind to accept that fact.

Another thing that worried Mark was the restlessness that took hold of Herb with the coming of warm weather. The job of looking after the cattle was still a chore. The grass was just beginning to show. Cows that were calving needed attention, and the hay, almost gone now, had to be carefully parceled out against the day when the grass would be up. But apparently Herb thought Mark could do the work by himself. Without giving any explanation, Herb would saddle up two or three times a week and ride into the hills and be gone until dark.

"He's out hunting Orry Andrews's body again," Mark told Ruth angrily. "He's like a man haunted by a ghost."

"Maybe he is haunted," Ruth said.

"But it's dangerous. He's been warned enough to stay off Cross Seven range. You've got to stop him."

"You think I can stop him?" Ruth shook her head. "Mark, you know I can't."

"But it's not right. When he's gone, I've got to do his work too."

"There was a time when you did it for Bronco Curtis," Ruth reminded him. "Do you regret coming back here?"

He took her into his arms and kissed her. "Not for a minute. You know that. But someday . . ."

"I know, darling," Ruth interrupted. "Someday we'll have our own ranch because we'll reach the place where this partnership won't work. I've known that all the time, and I think Dad has, too, but that *someday* hasn't come."

She reached out and took his hand and placed it against her swollen abdomen to let him feel the life that was stirring there. He grinned at her, embarrassed, for he knew she was right. He said: "Sometimes you're so smart you scare me. It's not that I'm sore about doing some of his work. I just don't want to see him killed. I like him."

"And he likes you, but, Mark, I don't think he can help himself. About hunting for Orry Andrews's body, I mean." She looked at him, a worry in her eyes that bothered him. Finally she said: "I love you so much it kind of hurts. Don't ever do the kind of crazy thing he's doing. You owe it to me and to our baby to stay alive."

"Why, honey," he said, "I aim to stay alive a long time. Until the day we celebrate our golden wedding anniversary."

But in spite of his light answer, her words made him uneasy. He thought about it a great deal after that, not certain that he knew exactly what she meant. He wondered if she was talking about Bronco. If Bronco killed Herb, Mark would have to go after Bronco. He would have to kill him if he could, regardless of what had once been between them. Any man who was a man would do the same. Ruth should know that, but he was afraid she didn't.

Maybe it was the kind of thing a woman never understood. If that day came, he would hurt her as he had never hurt her before, because it was something he could not keep from doing. When he recognized that, he understood the compulsion that drove Herb to go on looking for Orry Andrews's body. Ruth was right. Herb couldn't help himself. Maybe, Mark thought, if Ruth understood her father, she would understand him.

Mark put off going to town as long as he could, but there came a day when the salt and sugar were gone, and flour was down to half a sack. The roads were a loblolly of mud, so Mark took a pack horse. Herb had already left on one of his trips into the hills. When Mark was ready to go, Ruth kissed him, holding him hard as if not wanting to let him leave her.

Worried, he said: "Maybe I ought to stop by the fort and ask Missus Bolton to come and stay with you until the baby comes."

"For two months?" Ruth laughed. "You're being silly again."

He was, he thought as he rode away, but Ruth was pleased by his concern. It was only right and proper, he told himself, that a man should be concerned about his wife when she had her first baby. Maybe it was something a man never got over whether it was the first or the tenth.

By the time he reached Scott City, the stench was worse than it was on the Circle J. There weren't enough coyotes to clean the rotting flesh from the bones, and Mark wondered how the people who lived in the valley could stand it. He asked Cameron when he went into the store.

Cameron stared at Mark sourly. He had aged ten years in the few months since the last time Mark had seen him. Finally he said: "You can stand anything when you have to. What'll you have?"

Mark gave him the order. As he filled it, Cameron said: "Heard the news?" Mark shook his head, not knowing what news the store man referred to. Cameron went on: "Me 'n' Sharon got married a month ago. She wanted you to come to the wedding, but there wasn't any way to get word to you, traveling being like it's been. She always speaks well of you. Not like she does Curtis. God, how she hates that bastard."

Cameron cocked his head at Mark. "She claims Curtis got mad at her on account of her cooking and fired her, but I can't figure that out. She's a good cook. What's your notion about it?"

"I wasn't there when it happened," Mark said. "Looks like you'll have to take her story."

"Sure, sure," Cameron said quickly. "Only, I keep wondering what makes her hate Curtis like she does. Ain't natural, seems like, for her to hate a man so much just 'cause he fired her."

Something was eating on Cameron. Maybe he suspected the truth. But whether he did or not, he had married her and he'd better make the most of it. Mark said more sharply than he intended: "Sharon's a good woman, Cameron, a damned good woman. You're lucky to have her for a wife."

"I know it. Hell, I haven't had much to do since I got married, nobody moving around, the roads being like they are, so I've been laying in bed late and not opening the store till ten o'clock. She's a damned good woman for a fact." Then his face turned dark with suspicion, and he asked: "How'd you know?"

"I didn't mean it the way you're talking," Mark said. "She was good to me. That's all. Looked after me when I moved back to Cross Seven after being wounded at the fort. Bronco didn't treat her right, and I figure she's got reason to be sore at him."

"I see," Cameron said, the suspicion lingering.

Angry, Mark said: "You're a fool, Cameron. If you're going to accuse every man who comes in here of sleeping with her, you're headed for trouble, and that's what you'll deserve."

"All right, all right," Cameron said, and changed the subject with: "Heard about Nolan and Ardell?"

"They're hit hard," Mark said. "That's all I know."

"They're more'n hit hard. They're wiped out. Nolan had some gold buried in his yard, so he'll get out and re-stock, but I don't know about Ardell. If he can't borrow somewhere, he's a goner. Same with Curtis, only there's no doubt about him."

"Finished?"

Cameron nodded. "I guess they were lucky to save their horses. The crew's pulled out already. Gone south to one of Jacob Smith's Nevada ranches. Curtis is living alone. Nobody seems to know what he's going to do. Maybe he don't know himself."

"How'd you hear all this?"

"One of his buckaroos stopped here last week on his way out of the country and told me. This fellow wanted to go with the rest of the crew, but Gene Flagler wouldn't let him. He was the only man in the outfit who had been hired by Curtis."

"Who was he?"

"Abrams, I think he said. I didn't know him. Said Curtis owed him three months' wages, but he'll never get it. You know, that's a hell of a note. A lot of money for a cowhand to lose."

It was a hell of a note, Mark thought as he rode back to the Circle J. Bronco hadn't lasted very long. He'd ridden into the country with money in his pockets and a big dream. Now he'd leave with neither. And he would leave. He wasn't a man to stay and ride for Jacob Smith.

Mark intended to tell Ruth about Curtis as soon as he got home, but she came out of the house as he rode up. One look at her face told him something was wrong, so wrong that she wasn't in a mood to listen to gossip.

He swung down and took her hands. "What happened?"

"Dad found it," she said. "Curtis must have buried Orry in the bank of a gully where the dirt was soft. He threw some brush over the grave, but the bank caved in when the snow melted."

"What'd Herb find?"

"Bones. A skull with a bullet hole in it, and a Henry rifle that Dad knows belonged to Orry."

"It still doesn't prove Bronco did it," Mark said.

"Oh, Mark, aren't you ever going to face the truth?"

"I haven't tried and convicted Bronco the way Herb has."

She sighed. "I know. A man is innocent until he's proved guilty. Well, maybe he will be. Dad's gone to Cañon City to tell the sheriff."

Mark turned away, wondering what would happen if the sheriff believed Herb's story and came after Bronco? Or if Herb tried to help the sheriff arrest Bronco? Mark was sure of only one thing. Bronco would never submit to arrest.

Chapter Twenty-One

For more than a week neither Mark nor Ruth heard anything from Herb. The weather turned warm, and the grass, urged by the combined magic of a hot sun and a moist earth, came to life so fast that the hills and the valley floor that was above water turned a lush green in a matter of days.

"We'll have hay this year," Mark told Ruth. "If we just had more cattle . . ."

He doubted that Ruth heard. She heard very little these days, Mark thought. Her mind had fastened on her father, and Mark could not break through to her. At night she clung to him and cried, and all he could do was to hold her in his arms and tell her Herb would be all right, that it wasn't good for her or the baby to get worked up this way. But he couldn't touch her. He stayed awake every night long after Ruth had gone to sleep, and mentally flayed Herb Jackson.

No wagons had come over the pass from Cañon City this spring, and probably none would for another month. It was doubtful if a man could get through on a horse. Mark guessed that Herb had stopped at a ranch in the timber and borrowed snowshoes. That, Mark thought, was the reason it was taking Herb so long.

The whole thing was crazy. It had been from the first. Herb Jackson was a man of thought and ideas, a philosopher of sorts, an idealist. Why, then, had he become obsessed with the notion that Orry Andrews's murderer must be punished? And why, after finding the evidence, had he started for the county seat, knowing it would worry Ruth in her condition and knowing, too, that the sheriff didn't much care what happened in this distant end of the county?

No answer that made sense came to Mark. Having been utterly irrational, it occurred to him that Herb might do something that was still worse. If he couldn't get the sheriff to make a move, he might go directly to Cross Seven and try to kill Bronco. Being the kind of man he was, he would succeed only in getting himself killed. Maybe it had already happened.

Mark didn't mention this possibility to Ruth. The suspense was bad enough for her as it was. Then, on a Saturday morning nine days after Herb had left for Cañon City, a kid rode out from town with a note from Sharon Cameron.

> *Your father-in-law is back.*
> *Red Malone's here, too.*
> *He wants to see you.*

That was all, the words scrawled in pencil on a sheet torn from a cheap tablet. Mark stared at it for five minutes after the boy had started back down the slope toward Scott City. Why had Herb stayed in town, and why was Red Malone here, and why did he want to see Mark?

Mark didn't want to leave Ruth alone, but he had to. He walked slowly to the house, trying to mask his face against the turmoil that was boiling in him. He went into the kitchen where Ruth was baking bread.

"I think I'll take a ride," he said as casually as he could. "I've been working too hard. Or maybe it's just that I haven't been off the ranch for a long time."

She looked at him and nodded as if she knew he deserved some time off. He went on past her into the front room and, taking his gun belt off a peg near the door, buckled it around him. He was reaching for his rifle when she came into the room.

"Mark!"

She knows, he thought.

He turned to face her. "I thought I'd see if I could bring in some fresh meat. We sure can't afford to butcher a steer. Herb and me figure beef prices will be higher'n a cat's back this summer."

She believed him. At least she wanted to. He saw relief cross her face. He leaned the rifle against the wall, went to her, and put his arms around her, and kissed her.

"You'll be all right, won't you?" he asked. "I feel ornery about going off and leaving you, but I guess I've got cabin fever or something."

"I'll be all right," she said. "Wait a minute and I'll fix you a lunch."

"Don't bother. If I get hungry, I'll come home."

She stood in the doorway until he was in the saddle, then she waved at him and disappeared inside the house. He wasn't sure whether she believed him or not, so he had to act out the lie. He rode north toward the timber. He swung west as soon as he was hidden from the house and made a wide circle, wasting time he couldn't afford to waste.

He hoped he would find Herb in town, but if he had started for Cross Seven, Mark had to catch him before he got there. Then the thought came to Mark that Ruth deserved to know the truth, that he had been wrong to lie to her. It was something he had sworn he would never do, but he had. It was too late to change anything; he couldn't go back. Yet worry nagged at him all the way into town. If he and Herb were both killed today, and it could happen, what would become of Ruth?

There was some money. She would have the Circle J and a small herd that was worth a lot of money, or would be later in the spring when the soldiers at the fort needed beef. But who would look after her? Maybe she would get married again after the baby came. Or would she? He didn't know. All he knew was that he didn't want to die, that these months since the wedding were the nearest to being perfect of any in his life.

The instant Mark reached town, he sensed that something was wrong. A combination of warm weather and the end of the week had brought a dozen or more ranchers to town. They stood in little knots in front of the store and the saloon and the hotel, and, as he reined toward the saloon, they glanced at him, then pretended to look away, but he knew that they were furtively eyeing him.

Uncertainty added to the worry that was in Mark. Maybe Herb had left town, or maybe he was dead. Maybe Bronco had killed him and was still in town, knowing Mark would come.

He tied his horse, his gaze shifting from one group of men to another. He knew most of them, ranchers who had come to the Circle J begging for hay and had left cursing Herb and making dire threats. Probably every one of them wanted to see Herb dead. If Bronco had killed him and was waiting for Mark, he knew whose side they would be on.

Crazy, maybe, but the situation was crazy. These men were broke, and they would consider Bronco one of them because he was broke, too, if Cameron had told the straight of it. There was nothing else as tight as the fraternity of poverty, Mark thought.

He stepped back to loosen the cinch and took the opportunity to ease his gun out of the holster and gently lower it. Ridiculous to think he'd have trouble with these men, he told himself, yet it would have been ridiculous to think they would come to the Circle J and beg for hay that they knew Herb couldn't spare and then threaten his life when he refused.

Mark strode toward the saloon door, not thinking he would find Herb there, but knowing he had to look. Three men barred his way. They didn't move as he approached the batwings, but stood glowering at him. Mark laid his shoulder roughly against a man and shoved him half around and out of his way. Cursing, the man reached for his gun, but one of his friends grabbed his arm.

"Hold it, Dutch," the rancher said. "No sense of us buying into the ruckus."

Mark went on inside, not looking back. Matt Ardell stood at the bar, a filled shot glass in front of him. He looked old and beaten, much thinner than he had been in the fall, his skin hanging loosely from his jowls.

"Howdy, Mark," Ardell said. "I figured you'd be along."

Mark shook hands with him, asking: "How are you, Matt?"

"Busted," Ardell said. "I'll be picking bones before the summer's over."

"That bad?"

"It's that bad," Ardell said. "I'm going to Cañon City to see the bank. If I get turned down there, I'll go to Winnemucca. If I still get turned down, I'll go to Jacob Smith and make the same fool mistake that Bronco Curtis made."

"No, you won't," Mark said.

Ardell picked up his glass and gulped his drink, then set the glass back on the bar and grinned sheepishly at Mark. "No, I won't when it gets down to cases." He motioned toward the street. "But it's funny what happens to a man when he's cornered. Them ornery sons hate me and Dave Nolan and Herb because none of us would give 'em hay. But me 'n' Dave Nolan didn't have no hay to give 'em, and Herb did, so they hate him worse'n they do us."

"Where is Herb?"

"In bed in the hotel. Worn down to a nubbin. I stayed in town last night and was ready to pull out this morning when Herb rode in with a gent named Red Malone. It's hell getting over the pass on foot when you ain't used to snowshoes. Herb should have stayed the night at Jenner's ranch, where he left his horse, but he was on his way home and he wouldn't stop. When he got here, he fell flat on his face, so me 'n' Malone put him to bed. He'll be all right. Just needs some rest."

"Malone?"

"He's in the restaurant talking to Missus Cameron. She's the one who got the talk started about Bronco. She heard it from Malone. Seems he was hanging around the sheriff's office in Cañon City, trying to get news of Bronco, when Herb shows up with a skull and a Henry rifle he says belongs to Orry Andrews. He claims Bronco murdered Orry."

"What's it to everybody?" Mark asked angrily. "Do they love Bronco all of a sudden?"

Ardell shook his head. "No, it's just that they hate Herb. They'll get over it, give 'em time, but right now they figure Bronco's gonna plug you 'n' Herb, and they'll be tickled to see it."

Ardell reached for the bottle and filled his glass. He let it stand, staring at it. Finally he said: "Bronco's on his way here. Missus Cameron sent him word like she done you. Seems that Malone's gunning for him. Dunno why."

Mark turned from the bar.

Ardell asked: "Where you going, boy?"

"To see Malone. I hear he wants to see me."

"All right," Ardell said, "but come back here soon as you see Malone. Bronco's the one you've got to look out for. Herb's gonna go after Bronco when he wakes up. Malone says that's all he could talk about on the way back. The sheriff didn't believe his story. Wouldn't lift a finger, so Herb says he's gonna handle it hisself."

"What kind of word did Sharon send Bronco?"

"Dunno."

"I'll find out," Mark said, and left the saloon.

He went directly to the restaurant, feeling the eyes of every man on the street on him. Sharon met him in the door, her face grave. She said: "Mark, I sent for you because I thought you ought to know what's going on. This fellow, Malone, says he's got something he wants to tell you. Listen, but stay out of the fight. Malone's going to brace Bronco as soon as he shows up."

Mark stared at the woman, sensing the excitement that was in her. This was her way of getting Bronco killed, or so she hoped. But if it came to a fight between Bronco and Malone, she'd be disappointed. Bronco would take Malone. Mark was as sure of that as he could be sure of anything.

"How'd you get hooked up with Malone?" Mark asked.

"He got into town early this morning with Herb Jackson," she said. "Jackson was out on his feet, so . . ."

"I know," Mark interrupted. "Ardell told me."

"Well, Malone came in for his breakfast and started talking. He gave me the whole yarn. I egged him on some, all right. I found a man to go after Bronco, and I figure he'll come a-running."

"I guess that's what you want."

"You're damned right it is," she shot back at him. "But it's your father-in-law I'm worried about. If Malone don't get Bronco, there'll be hell to pay. I know what Bronco thinks of Herb Jackson. He told me a dozen times that, if Jackson ever pushed that Orry Andrews business, he'd plug him. Well, now everybody in town knows that Jackson found the evidence he's been looking for, so Bronco won't have no choice."

Mark looked past her at Malone, who had stepped out of the kitchen. The scene in Prineville came back to Mark as if it had been yesterday; he remembered exactly how Malone looked, and when Malone said—"Howdy, Kelton."—Mark remembered the voice.

Mark said: "I'm going to kill you, Malone. You knew that when you came here, didn't you?"

"No, I don't think you will, sonny," Malone said easily. "You see, you got things mixed up. It was Bronco Curtis who murdered your parents, not me."

Chapter Twenty-Two

For a moment Mark stood staring at Malone, stupefied. The possibility that Bronco had killed his parents had occurred to Mark, but he had never given it serious thought, partly because stabbing two people to death when they were sleeping was not Bronco's way, particularly when one was a woman, but mostly because it was inconceivable that a man would have thrown in with the son of two people he had just murdered. Oh, he might have taken him as far as the Baxes' place, or even to Prineville, but to have "nursed a wet-nosed kid" for the entire summer was more than Bronco or any man guilty of murder would have done.

Now that he faced Malone, the old, poignant memories flocked back into Mark's mind: the discovery that his parents were dead, his headlong run and exhaustion, Bronco's coming along the road and taking him to the Baxes Ranch, the simple funeral, and seeing Malone in Prineville and recognizing his voice.

The edge of his grief had been blunted long ago. He had his own life now: a wife, a baby that was on the way, and the knowledge that there was nothing he could do to change what had happened. Still, the need to punish a terrible crime that had been committed almost two years before was in Mark, and it would continue to be in him as long as the murderer went unpunished.

Maybe he couldn't prove Malone had done it any more than Herb Jackson could prove that Bronco Curtis had killed Orry Andrews, prove it conclusively so that Malone would be convicted in court and hanged. But he knew, and now, staring at

189

Malone, Mark realized that this same kind of haunting knowledge had been in Herb Jackson's mind all this while, driving him back onto Cross Seven range time after time.

The moment of shock passed. Mark said: "You're a liar. I don't know why you're here. I wasn't going to hunt you, because I didn't know where you were." He took a long breath, stepping away from Sharon as he nodded at Malone. "But you are here, and I'm going to kill you."

"Hold on, boy," Malone said. "I'm not after you. It's Curtis I want. I've been looking for him nigh onto two years, and now, by God, I've run him down and I'll kill him."

Sharon grabbed Mark's right arm. "Let him talk, Mark. I didn't send for you to fight him. All I wanted was for you to hear what he had to say before he plugged Bronco or Bronco got him."

Malone was ready to draw if Mark forced a fight. Mark read it in the redhead's eyes, in the way he stood, right hand close to gun butt. "All right," Mark said. "I'll listen, but it won't make any difference. Talk, and then I'll kill you."

Malone laughed. "Sonny, you're talking like a fool. You won't kill me. You'll kill Bronco Curtis."

"That why you want to tell me your cock-and-bull story?" Mark asked. "You figure I'll take Bronco on and save you the trouble?"

"It's a good reason," Malone said blandly. "It don't make no difference to me whether you do it, or I do, but I can tell you one thing. Bronco Curtis won't leave this burg alive. He double-crossed me. Let Curtis do it and so will the next man. Now you ready to listen?"

"I said I was."

"All right. This is the way it was. Bronco got into a high-stakes poker game in Albany. It lasted thirty-six hours. I never saw the beat of it. When it was over, he was broke. Didn't worry him none because we'd knocked over a couple of banks and a few stagecoaches, so we knew we could fill our pockets again, but Bronco had heard about your pa selling his farm for $8,000 and going to central Oregon to buy a ranch, so he says we'll tag along. When the sign's right, we'll lift the *dinero*. Be easier than tackling a bank or a stage.

"You didn't know it, but we trailed you all the way over the Santiam Pass and clean to the Deschutes. We waited till your folks got there so we'd be out of Linn County and wouldn't have the Albany sheriff on our tail. Bronco got into the wagon while you and your folks was sleeping. He killed 'em. Wasn't me."

"It was you I caught coming out of the wagon!" Mark shouted. "You had the metal box. I heard your voice. You had a beard. Bronco didn't."

"Sure, it was me you caught coming out of the wagon," Malone said, "but what you didn't know was that Bronco had already been in the wagon and killed both of 'em. He claimed he couldn't find the box, so I got inside and I found it. That's why I'm gunning for him. He'd found the box all right and took most of the *dinero*. When we opened it later on, there wasn't but about $2,000. Bronco cussed a blue streak and claimed we'd heard a bunch of lies about what your pa got for his farm. Like a fool I believed him. Didn't know any difference till I got to The Dalles and read a paper. Then I knowed he'd cheated me, but by then he'd disappeared. Been looking for him ever since. I wintered in Cañon City and heard what Jackson had to say. That's why I'm here."

"You're still lying," Mark said bitterly. "You're so damned yellow you're afraid to jump Bronco. You figure I'll do it and save your hide."

Malone laughed again, a short, barking sound. "Kid, I never ducked a fight in my life, and I sure ain't gonna duck one with Bronco, but, if you think you've got a better claim to him than I have, you can have first chance. Trouble is, you ain't man enough to take him, so you'd better work out a scheme with Jackson to ship-saw Bronco when he shows up."

Mark still believed Malone was lying, but now there was doubt in him, just enough doubt to keep him from pulling his gun. So he stood there, staring at Malone and hating him because by his own admission he had helped rob Mark's parents and had shared in the results of that robbery. Then Mark thought about the money Bronco had been carrying. He had said it had come from a poker game, exactly the opposite to Malone's story.

Apparently Sharon had been thinking the same thing. She asked: "Mark, how much money did Bronco have when he first hooked up with you? Could it have been $7,000?"

"He never told me," Mark said, "so I don't know, but I don't think it was nearly that much. All I know is that he had $3,000 to give Orry Andrews for Cross Seven."

"Which he got back from Andrews when he murdered him," Malone said.

"We don't know he murdered Andrews," Mark said stubbornly. "He sure didn't have much after he bought the ranch."

"That's where you're making your mistake, Mark," Sharon said. "He had to have some money. He put up new buildings. Bought more horses. Had to pay a big crew once Jacob Smith sent a herd north with Gene Flagler."

"Smith loaned him the money," Mark said.

"Oh, no!" Sharon cried. "Not Jacob Smith. He'd risk a herd of cattle just to get his toehold up here that he'd been wanting, but Bronco spent thousands of dollars putting up those buildings and buying horses and mowers and the rest of that stuff. Jacob's too tight to gamble both money and cattle. Bronco had it, Mark. I don't know how he got it, but he had it."

Now the doubt grew in Mark, grew and festered until he knew he had to face Bronco, had to face him and ask questions.

He didn't believe Bronco would lie. If he did, Mark thought he would know it.

"All right," Mark said finally, "I've listened and I'll jump Bronco when he shows up." He jabbed a forefinger at Malone. "But don't leave town. Sharon and I heard you admit you helped rob my parents. You'll go to jail for it, or I'll kill you."

"You can try," Malone said smugly. "I won't leave town. You can count on that. Now, if I was you, I'd get Jackson to help me. Bronco's a bad one. You can't take him by yourself."

Mark wheeled and left the restaurant. Malone's game was plain enough. He was a coward just as Mark had said. He had it figured out how to get Bronco killed without running any risk himself. With Herb Jackson feeling the way he did about Bronco, and with Mark's natural desire to avenge his parents' murder, Malone was confident Mark would take his suggestion and team up with Herb to kill Bronco without giving him a chance.

To hell with Malone, Mark thought as he returned to the saloon. He'd talk to Bronco. That was all. He wasn't sure what he'd say, but he had to try.

The men were still bunched along the street just as they had been, their eyes following Mark as he strode toward the saloon. The ones in front of the batwings hadn't moved. As Mark walked past them, one of them said something. It was the same man he had pushed out of his way when he had first gone into the saloon. Mark wasn't sure what the man said, but judging from the tone, the rancher was hungry for a fight. Mark hesitated, then went inside. At the moment it wasn't important.

The saloon was empty except for the bartender and Matt Ardell. Ardell's eyes were questioning. Mark asked: "Seen Herb?"

"No."

"If he comes in, get him back outside. I want to talk to Bronco alone. Soon as he rides in, ask him to come inside."

"I'll try," Ardell said.

"Keep everybody else out."

"Now hold on, Kelton," the bartender said. "You can't keep customers . . ."

"I can and I will," Mark said. "After this is over, you'll sell more whiskey than you've sold all year. Matt, this is important."

"I said I'd try." Ardell followed Mark to a table. When Mark sat down facing the batwings, Ardell asked: "What's up?"

"Malone says Bronco murdered my parents two years ago," Mark said. "I don't believe it. I think Malone did it, but I've got to talk to Bronco."

"You've got a wife," Ardell said. "Bronco's a killer. Don't forget what happened at the fort during the Indian trouble."

"I haven't, and I haven't forgotten Ruth, either," Mark said, "but this is something I've got to do."

Ardell nodded as if he understood. He walked to the front window and stood looking into the street.

Mark drew his gun and laid it across his lap. He sat there, knowing he could not let himself think of Ruth or the baby. Or of his parents. Or of how much he owed Bronco and the dreams they once had shared. Or of death and the ethics of a fair fight. If Bronco got tangled in his own lies and convicted himself, Mark would shoot him under the table. It would not be murder; it would be a long-delayed execution.

He remembered something Herb had said once, something Mark had forgotten but that now returned to his mind. *A man can't escape that which is destined to be.*

He sat staring at the green table top as the long minutes dragged out, wondering if fate had decreed that he must die under Bronco Curtis's gun.

Chapter Twenty-Three

Mark had no idea how long he sat at the table. His mind simply had no capacity to judge time. He didn't even think about it. He would wait if it took all day. His only fear was that Herb Jackson might waken from his sleep of exhaustion before Bronco got here.

The saloon man remained behind the bar, glowering at Mark. Matt stood at the window, watching. Then without glancing around, he said: "Bronco's here."

"Fetch him in," Mark said.

Ardell turned, hesitating, staring at Mark as if mentally searching for some way to stop this whole thing. Then he shrugged and stepping into the street, called: "Bronco!"

There was some talk Mark couldn't hear, then Bronco came through the door and strode directly to Mark's table. Ardell followed for three steps before he veered off toward the bar, where he stood, watching.

This was the first time Mark had seen Bronco since last fall when he had left Cross Seven with his jag of steers to join the Triangle R's drive to the railroad. Mark was shocked. Bronco carried himself as coldly confident as ever, shoulders squared, back straight, chin jutting forward, but there the resemblance to the old Bronco Curtis ended. His clothes were ragged, he hadn't shaved for two weeks, there was a deep network of lines around his eyes, and he was whittled down to hide and bone.

He had the wolf look about him again, just as he'd had two years ago during the summer Mark had ridden with him, but now he didn't even have a whelp to ride beside him. A solitary he-wolf who had withdrawn from the pack, Bronco Curtis was more dangerous than he had ever been in his life.

Mark intended to ask immediately what part Bronco had had in the murder and robbery of his parents, but before he opened his mouth, Bronco said: "I fired that bitch the minute I got back and found out you'd left. I don't blame you for wanting to get married, but why'n hell didn't you come back after I got rid of Sharon?"

Mark stared up at Bronco, who stood, spread-legged, on the other side of the table, scowling. He was not a man who could be soft or gentle about anything; this was as near as he could come, but it seemed to Mark that, in spite of the rough words and tone, Bronco was trying to say that he had missed Mark. Or maybe it was what Mark wanted to think Bronco was trying to say. He wasn't sure.

"I told you before you left I was pulling out," Mark said. "It wasn't because of Sharon."

"The hell it wasn't," Bronco said. "You ain't like me, wanting to take any woman any time you can get into bed with her. You were thinking of Ruth, and it was too damned tough to stay there with Sharon wanting to crawl in with you, so you had to leave. All winter I thought you'd come riding back, but, by God, you never did."

"You've got things wrong," Mark said. "Maybe you've forgotten how it was. When we hit this valley, you were calling me your partner. It was the same the first winter we were on Cross Seven, but when I came back after the Indian trouble, you'd thrown in with Jacob Smith. From then on I was just a chore boy. I stayed home and hauled manure. I wasn't even good enough to ride with the crew."

"Why, hell, boy, I didn't know . . ."

"Yes, Bronco, you knew, all right. I asked you for wages enough times. You turned me down. I got married without a cent. Herb Jackson made me a real partner when I first got to the Circle J. We sold a few head of steers to the fort, and he split the money with me. If it hadn't been for that, I wouldn't have had enough money to buy my wife a wedding ring."

Bronco blinked as if surprised. Maybe he hadn't thought about it, Mark told himself, thinking about himself as much as he did. Mark said: "I'm going to ask you a question. I want a straight answer. I've got my gun on my lap. If you lie to me, I'll kill you. Why did you run herd on me that first summer, Bronco?"

Bronco laughed. "You won't kill me for the same reason that you're the only man alive I wouldn't kill." Then the laughter fled from his bearded face. "What are you talking that way for?"

"Answer my question."

"That why Matt called me in here?"

"That's right."

"Where's Red Malone?"

"In the restaurant with Sharon."

"I might have knowed. So he got together with that bitch first thing. What'd he tell you?"

"Answer my question, Bronco."

"All right, damn it. I found you sitting beside the road. You were big enough to be a man, but you wasn't. You didn't know how far was up. If I hadn't taken a hand, Malone would have killed you in Prineville, and you know it."

"Yes, I know it, but you still haven't answered my question."

"'Cause I felt sorry for you. That's why. You'd have starved to death, and the coyotes would have picked your bones clean. You were mighty god-damned helpless. I'd have picked up a starving pup for the same reason."

"But you wouldn't have kept him," Mark said. "I guess that's what I'm trying to ask. I'm grateful for what you did, but that's not going to keep me from shooting you for killing my parents."

"For what?" Bronco shouted. "My God, boy, I didn't kill your folks. I didn't even know they were dead till I found you and you told me. I didn't believe it even then. I had to go back and see for myself."

He's not lying, Mark thought. Still, what he'd said about being sorry for Mark wasn't good enough. Bronco Curtis wasn't a man to load himself with a helpless parasite of a boy because he felt sorry for him.

Speaking slowly, Mark said: "Red Malone says you were in the wagon before he went in. He says you murdered my parents, took most of the money, claimed you couldn't find the box, and got out. Then he crawled in and found it."

Bronco didn't move for a time. He stood motionlessly, as coldly furious as Mark had ever seen him, a pulse pounding in his temple, the corners of his mouth quivering. When he did speak, his words were barely audible: "I never thought you'd believe that bastard."

"I don't believe all he said. He admitted helping rob my folks, and I aim to take care of him, but right now I'm asking you."

"I've got nothing to say," Bronco shot back. "If you don't know me well enough by now to know I wouldn't stab a man and woman to death when they're asleep, then you wouldn't believe a word I said. But I will tell you why I ran herd on you that summer. I felt sorry for you like I said, then I got to liking you. You had sand in your craw. I found that out that time in Nevada. I saw it more'n once after we got here. Like with them Paiutes. I told you a man looked out for me once. I couldn't pay him back, but I could do something for you. Maybe you'll find a kid someday to pay me back."

He turned and strode toward the batwings.

Mark said sharply: "One more thing, Bronco."

Bronco wheeled back to face him. "I'm going to look for Malone. I'll shut his lying mouth for good, and I'll fix that damned bitch of a Sharon so she'll be sorry she ever listened to Malone."

"They'll wait," Mark said. "Both of them."

He hesitated, believing what Bronco had said. He was a selfish man, but it was possible he had honestly liked Mark, and it was possible he had felt a debt to a man who had once looked out for him. But there was the trouble with Herb Jackson, and this was the time to have it out.

"Well?" Bronco asked.

"Heard about Herb Jackson?"

"What about him?"

"He found some human bones on Cross Seven range that he says are what's left of Orry Andrews. Also a Henry rifle he recognizes. He's been in Cañon City with his evidence and charged you with the murder, but the sheriff won't do anything. Herb's back, and he's going to get you, he says."

Bronco returned to where Mark sat, the fury strangely gone from him. He put his hands on the edge of the table. He said slowly: "Then Jackson's a dead man. I'm sorry about that for your sake, but he knows what I'll do if he keeps pushing that lie of his at me. I'll kill him. I was willing to let him alone if he'd let me alone, but I reckon he won't do that."

"No, he won't," Mark said. "I can't let you kill him, Bronco."

"What do you want me to do?" Bronco demanded. "Stand still while he fills my hide full of holes? I won't do that. Not even for you, boy."

"He's my father-in-law," Mark said.

Mark's finger tightened on the trigger of the gun he held under the table. He stared across the green top at Bronco, feeling that what he was going to do was terribly wrong, but he knew

Bronco was bound to shoot Herb because Herb wouldn't let the Orry Andrews's business drop. Mark couldn't let Bronco do it.

"Father-in-law or not," Bronco said, "I don't aim to stand here and let you . . ."

Bronco slammed the table hard against Mark, sending him sprawling backward onto the floor, the gun going off as he fell. Then Bronco was on top of him, his knees driving into Mark's belly, knocking breath out of him. He twisted the gun out of Mark's hand, rolled off, and got to his feet. Then he stood looking down, the gun lined on Mark's chest.

"You were fixing to shoot me under the table," Bronco said as if he could not understand it. "But you ain't yellow, boy. I've lived with you too long to think you are."

Mark didn't say anything.

"You knew you couldn't outdraw me," Bronco went on, "so you figured this was the only way to keep me from beefing Herb Jackson. That it?"

"That's it," Mark said. "If you kill Herb, I'll hunt you down and I'll shoot you, Bronco. That's a promise."

Bronco backed toward the batwings, his lean face turned bitter. "If you try it, I'll have to kill you, too, Mark, and that's the last thing I want to do."

He kept on backing toward the door, and it came to Mark in a flashing insight of truth that avenging his parents' death was not as important as he had thought, but keeping Herb Jackson alive was.

"I hear you're broke, Bronco," Mark said. "Leave the country. Herb can't hurt you if he can't find you."

Bronco slipped Mark's gun under his waistband. He said: "I'm broke, but I'll get started again. I'm not leaving the country, boy. Not for you or Herb Jackson or anyone." He went on toward the batwings, then paused. "I'm going after Malone. Then I'm leaving town. If Jackson comes after me, I'll do what I have to do to save my life. Tell him that."

He wheeled and pushed the batwings apart with his hands and went on out into the sunlight. Jackson would go after him, Mark knew. There was nothing he could do to stop Jackson. He got up and walked toward the door, not seeing either the bartender or Matt Ardell. Then, just two steps from the door, he heard the sudden, slamming sound of gunfire in the street.

Chapter Twenty-Four

Mark charged through the swinging doors. Bronco was on his hands and knees, struggling to get up. Failing, he fell flat on his stomach. The three men who had been standing near the door were diving frantically for cover. Malone stood in front of Sharon's restaurant, a smoking gun in his hand. Mark heard Sharon's scream, a high, sustained sound that went on and on as if it would never stop, just as it seemed this terrible moment would never stop.

Apparently Malone had been waiting for Bronco to come through the saloon door so he could kill him if Mark didn't.

Mark stooped and jerked his gun from Bronco's waistband. As he straightened, Malone threw a shot at him, the bullet splintering the top of one of the swing doors behind Mark. Then Mark saw why Malone had missed. Sharon had darted out of the restaurant and grabbed Malone's right arm. He hit her with his left hand, a hard blow that knocked her sprawling into the street. Then he whirled and disappeared into the restaurant.

Mark ran across the street. As he raced past Sharon, she screamed: "He'll kill you, Mark! Let him go!"

But that was something he could not do. He ran through the door and past the counter and on into the kitchen, expecting Malone to make a stand, but the man wasn't in sight. Mark charged on into the weed-covered lot.

As Mark cleared the back door, he glimpsed Malone running west. Mark fired and missed, then Malone was out of sight around the corner of the next building, running in a headlong gait as if his only concern was to get away.

Mark sprinted after the fugitive, wondering why he didn't make a fight out of it. As Mark rounded the corner of the next building, he saw that Malone was almost across the street, headed for the livery stable.

Mark stopped and brought up his gun, intending to shoot the man squarely between the shoulder blades. Malone was the one who had murdered his parents, not Bronco. It was Malone's way, just as shooting Bronco down without giving him a chance was Malone's way. Running now, instead of facing Mark, was part of the same pattern of behavior.

Mark squeezed off a shot just as Malone reached the archway of the stable, but the bullet was low. It caught Malone in the right thigh, knocking his leg out from under him as effectively as if he'd stumbled over a taut rope. Mark ran across the street, yelling: "I'll kill you if you try to use your gun!"

Cornered and unable to run, Malone rolled over on his left side. He still held his gun. He threw a shot that kicked up dust in front of Mark. Then, seeing he had missed, he screamed: "Don't shoot! Don't shoot!"

But he was too late. Mark's finger was tight against the trigger. He could not have stopped the impulse even if he had wanted to. He heard the shot and felt the hard buck of the gun against his palm, and through the drifting cloud of smoke he saw Malone's head jerk, then Malone collapsed into the barn litter that covered the ground in the archway.

Mark walked to the man, his gun still covering him. When he reached Malone, he holstered the gun. Malone had been killed instantly, the bullet hitting him just below the nose. If Bronco was dead, Mark would never know the full truth about his parents' deaths, about Bronco's part in it. But Malone had lied. Of that Mark was sure.

For a moment he stood, staring down at the dead man, seeing again in his mind the bodies of his parents as he had found them that morning on the Deschutes, remembering the stark terror that had been in him. He had avenged their deaths, for whatever good that was. At least Red Malone would not murder again, and, if Bronco was dead, Herb Jackson would find peace at last.

As Mark turned away, the street suddenly became alive. Men who had dived for cover now appeared. Cameron ran out of his store. Sharon had crossed to where Bronco lay in front of the saloon, and Herb Jackson, awakened by the shooting, stumbled out of the hotel, looking as if he were not yet fully awake.

Matt Ardell was bending over Bronco. He straightened and, jerking a hand in Mark's direction, called: "Bronco's hard hit, Mark. He wants to talk to you."

Mark ran toward the saloon. As he passed Jackson, he paused to say: "Malone shot Bronco Curtis, and I shot Malone." He went on, and Jackson, shocked awake, followed.

By the time they reached the saloon, Bronco had been carried inside and laid on a cot in a back room. Sharon was kneeling beside him, crying: "I'm to blame, I'm to blame." She was saying it over and over, unable to stop until Matt Ardell slapped her on the side of the face. She stopped, the blow returning her to sanity, but she remained on her knees, sobbing.

Ardell motioned for Mark to come close to the cot. He said: "Bronco ain't got long, and he's worried about not having time to tell you something."

Mark stood at Bronco's head. "I'm here, Bronco."

Bronco's right hand clutched his belly, blood seeping through his fingers. He raised his left hand, saying: "It's dark, boy. I can't see you."

Mark took his hand. "I'm here beside you, Bronco."

"I've got to tell you how it was," Bronco said. "You'll believe me now?"

"I'll believe you."

"I planned the robbery," Bronco said. "Heard about your pa selling his farm. Me 'n' Malone followed your wagon, but I never aimed to hurt your folks. I stayed outside to watch, figuring you'd wake up and tackle one of us. I knew Malone would kill you if you did, so I sent him into the wagon to get the money. If your folks woke up, he was to knock 'em out."

Bronco stopped until a paroxysm of pain passed. He went on, his voice so low that Mark had to bend over him to hear. "I was the one who hit you. Malone tripped as he started to run. He fell and dropped the box. I picked it up, and we both ran. I took most of the money without him knowing it. When we counted it later, there was only a couple of thousand, and I cussed big, saying we'd been fooled. We got back to our camp and pulled out. We split up in case a posse took after us. I thought he was going to The Dalles. I didn't figure on running into him in Prineville."

He stopped again, biting his lower lip so hard he brought blood. He said: "It's getting damned dark."

For a moment Mark thought he was gone, then he whispered: "I didn't know who you were when I found you beside the road. I'd just seen you at a distance. I didn't believe you when you said your folks were dead. Not till I went back and found 'em. I couldn't let you starve. After we got over here, I aimed to make you my partner 'cause it was your money I was using. I never wanted you to leave Cross Seven. I liked you. Didn't know how you really felt . . . 'bout being chore boy. Move back onto it. . . . It's yours by right. . . . Don't let Jacob Smith . . . have . . . it."

He tried to say something else. His lips moved, and Mark thought he wasn't going to get it said, then the words came slowly: "I killed Orry Andrews. Didn't aim to. Had to have the money back I paid him to buy stock. I took it away from him. He tried to kill me. . . . I shot . . . him in self-defense."

His hand in Mark's went slack. A moment later he was dead. Mark laid Bronco's hand across his chest, glanced at Sharon who was still on her knees, and turned away, wondering what would happen between her and Cameron.

She had hated Bronco because he had sent her away, but now she regretted what had happened, and she would blame herself as long as she lived. If Cameron hadn't been sure about her before, and about how she had felt toward Bronco, he would be now.

Mark went on through the saloon to the street, not doubting what Bronco had told him, for the man had known he was dying. He had been mostly bad, but not as bad as Herb Jackson believed. But bad or good, Mark could never forget what Bronco Curtis had done for him.

Orry Andrews? Mark believed Bronco had told the truth about that, too, and remembered thinking it could have been that way. Bronco had had an obsession about the ranch; it had been the only important thing in the world to him. Not that the killing or even the robbery could be overlooked, but it made the actions of a man understandable, a man who was a violent mixture of both good and bad.

Herb Jackson caught up with Mark on the saloon porch. "Wait till I get my horse from the livery stable. I'll ride home with you."

"Sure," Mark said.

"Hold on!" Matt Ardell called, and joined them on the porch. He looked at Jackson. "Satisfied, Herb?"

"I'm satisfied," Jackson said. "He's paid for his crimes." He turned to Mark. "It's a pet belief of mine that good and evil are rewarded in their proper fashion, somewhere, sometime."

Mark did not believe it, so he simply nodded and remained silent.

Ardell said: "We all heard Curtis. Cross Seven is yours, Mark. What are you going to do?"

"I don't know," Mark said. "Chances are Jacob Smith will claim it."

"Of course he will," Ardell said, "but he's got to be stopped, or he'll wind up owning the whole valley once he gets his toe in the door at Cross Seven. I'm going to talk to Dave Nolan and John Runyan. They know how it is as well as I do. I'll borrow money somewhere and get started again. I don't know how, but I will. We'll help you stock Cross Seven. It's in your interest, too, Herb. You need a friendly neighbor to the east of you."

"It'll mean a fight with Smith," Jackson said.

Ardell nodded. "You bet it will, but there's one thing about your son-in-law. He won't back away from a fight."

"No," Jackson agreed. "I've known that for quite a while."

"How about it, Mark?" Ardell asked. "Will you try it if we back you?"

"I'll try it," Mark said.

"Good," Ardell said, and turned into the saloon.

Mark tightened the cinch and untied his horse, then stepped into the saddle, feeling the eyes of the men who had gathered again into little knots along the street. He rode slowly out of town, thinking this had not gone the way they had expected. Some would survive, some would leave, but in time those who remained would forget their anger with Herb for his refusal to sell hay and would be neighborly again.

Presently Jackson caught up with him, and they rode together. Jackson said: "I'm a free man now. I know what you think of me on account of the way I've been about Orry's murder, but it's something I can't explain."

"Don't try," Mark said. "I know how it was."

Jackson looked at him in surprise. "How can you?"

"I left Ruth alone when I heard Malone was in town," Mark said. "I didn't want to. I lied to her because I didn't think she'd understand. But I was wrong. I should have told her the truth. This is something she's got to understand about a man."

"Yes," Jackson said. "I think she will, in time." He cleared his throat, then he said: "Mark, I hate to have you and Ruth leave the Circle J, and, if it doesn't work out, I hope you'll always feel free to come back, but you and I are different. I wouldn't cast you in my mold if I could. You want to grow and I'd only hold you back, so go ahead and make your try at Cross Seven. Living is filled with fighting any way you look at it. I guess there's no sense in trying to avoid it. I think you'll lick Jacob Smith."

"I aim to," Mark said, glancing at Jackson's face. He'd thought he knew this strange, gentle man, but he had underestimated his understanding just as, he realized, he had underestimated Ruth's. He added: "Thanks, Herb."

He touched up his horse and rode on toward the Circle J, and Ruth.

THE END

About the Author

Wayne D. Overholser won three Spur Awards from the Western Writers of America and has a long list of fine Western titles to his credit. He was born in Pomeroy, Washington, and attended the University of Montana, University of Oregon, and the University of Southern California before becoming a public schoolteacher and principal in various Oregon communities. He began writing for Western pulp magazines in 1936 and within a couple of years was a regular contributor to Street & Smith's *Western Story Magazine* and Fiction House's *Lariat Story Magazine*. *Buckaroo's Code* (1947) was his first Western novel and remains one of his best. In the 1950s and 1960s, having retired from academic work to concentrate on writing, he would publish as many as four books a year under his own name or a pseudonym, most prominently as Joseph Wayne. *The Violent Land* (1954), *The Lone Deputy* (1957), *The Bitter Night* (1961), and *Riders of the Sundowns* (1997) are among the finest of the Overholser titles. *The Sweet and Bitter Land* (1950), *Bunch Grass* (1955), and *Land of Promises* (1962) are among the best Joseph Wayne titles, and *Law Man* (1953) is a most rewarding novel under the Lee Leighton pseudonym. Overholser's Western novels, whatever the byline, are based on a solid knowledge of the history and customs of the nineteenth-century West, particularly when set in his two favorite Western states, Oregon and Colorado. Many of his novels are first-person narratives, a technique that tends to bring an added dimension of vividness to the frontier experiences of his narrators and frequently, as in *Cast a Long Shadow* (1957), the female characters one encounters are among the most memorable. He wrote his numerous novels with a consistent skill and an uncommon sensitivity to the depths of human character. Almost invariably, his stories weave a spell of their own with their scenes and images of social and economic forces often in conflict and the diverse ways of life and personalities that made the American Western frontier so unique a time and place in human history.